W9-AHZ-144

"Miss Weldon, I know why you're here."

Vargen went on in his slightly accented tones, "I know the secret reason you have come to Avala."

Shelley's instinct was to flee from this dangerous-looking man, but she could not move.

"I know that you are here to buy the Hotel Catalina, and I also know what your father will do if you fail," Vargen continued. "You should know that I now own the hotel, and unless you agree to my proposition—"

"Proposition?" Shelley gasped.

He paused, turning slowly. "I need a wife. It is essential for me to marry within seven days. If you agree, the Hotel Catalina is yours. If not ...."

An image of Shelley's father, furious, flashed before her eyes, almost stopping her from shouting, "You're mad, Vargen Gilev! Get out!"

Other titles by
MARY WIBBERLEY
IN HARLEQUIN ROMANCES

1924—THE DARK ISLE
1935—THAT MAN BRYCE
1968—THE WILDERNESS HUT
1994—THE WHISPERING GATE
2031—THE MOON-DANCERS
2059—THE SILVER LINK
2085—DARK VENTURER
2105—WILDCAT TAMED
2136—DAUGHTER OF THE SUN
2147—WILD GOOSE
2177—LORD OF THE ISLAND
2221—THE TAMING OF TAMSIN
2245—WITCHWOOD
2267—LOVE'S SWEET REVENGE
2277—THE DARK WARRIOR
2298—RUNAWAY MARRIAGE
2316—WITH THIS RING
2340—A DANGEROUS MAN

Other titles by
MARY WIBBERLEY
IN HARLEQUIN PRESENTS

 89—THE SNOW ON THE HILLS
129—THE MAN AT LA VALAISE
348—SAVAGE LOVE
366—SAVAGE POSSESSION

Many of these titles are available at your local bookseller.

For a free catalogue listing all available Harlequin Romances,
send your name and address to:

HARLEQUIN READER SERVICE,
M.P.O. Box 707, Niagara Falls, N.Y. 14302
Canadian address: Stratford, Ontario, Canada N5A 6W2

Dangerous Marriage

by

MARY WIBBERLEY

Harlequin Books

TORONTO • LONDON • LOS ANGELES • AMSTERDAM
SYDNEY • HAMBURG • PARIS • STOCKHOLM • ATHENS • TOKYO

Original hardcover edition published in 1980
by Mills & Boon Limited
ISBN 0-373-02364-2
Harlequin edition published October 1980

Copyright © 1980 by Mary Wibberley.
Philippine copyright 1980. Australian copyright 1980.

All rights reserved. Except for use in any review, the reproduction or utilization
of this work in whole or in part in any form by any electronic, mechanical or
other means, now known or hereafter invented, including xerography,
photocopying and recording, or in any information storage or retrieval system,
is forbidden without the permission of the publisher. All the characters in this
book have no existence outside the imagination of the author and have no
relation whatsoever to anyone bearing the same name or names. They are not
even distantly inspired by any individual known or unknown to the author, and
all the incidents are pure invention.

The Harlequin trademark, consisting of the word HARLEQUIN and the
portrayal of a Harlequin, is registered in the United States Patent Office and
in the Canada Trade Marks Office.

Printed in the U.S.A.

CHAPTER ONE

THE man had been following her all morning, Shelley was sure of that. She had only caught distant glimpses of him as she had wandered round the market place, and the older part of Avala, but they had been enough. He was quite unmistakable, tall, dark and lean. She hadn't seen him close to—until now. She stood disbelieving in the foyer of the hotel where she was staying and watched as he walked in, through the swing doors, and across to the reception desk. He had a compelling face, a strikingly dark tanned, ruthless face, hawklike profile, high cheekbones, thick black hair. Then he turned and looked at her as if aware of her regard, and she saw tawny gold eyes piercing her before he turned away as if in silent dismissal, and spoke to the desk clerk.

Shelley experienced a brief helpless anger, felt the colour come into her cheeks, and for a moment didn't know what to do next. Escape? But to where? She was staying here. And she didn't want him following her to her room, or knowing her room number, which he would if she went over for her key now. She sat down on a long cane settee to look for the postcards she had bought. She had intended writing them in the foyer, posting them in the letter box near the swing doors, and then going up for a shower. She saw no reason to change her plans because of a disturbing stranger. If he was still in the foyer when she had done the cards, she would wait.

He was still talking to the clerk, and they were laugh-

ing. She opened her handbag and took out the five postcards with a steady hand. Men had followed her before,
she was used to it in England—but here was different,
very different, several thousand miles from home and
completely alone, and here for a purpose that only she
and her father knew. It was important, until after the
auction in two days, that no one else should know or
guess the reason for her holiday in Avala. She could
not, must not, let her father down. To do so would be
unthinkable, and his anger was a force that she had
learned, over the years, to avoid at all costs.

She looked down at the gaudy pictures of the island
of Avala, her eyes blurring with sudden tears. Her
father had always wanted a son. He had never really
forgiven her for being born a girl, and in some strange
way she had been trying to please him, to make him
accept her, ever since. This was her first big test. Failure
would be unthinkable. For the first time ever he was
relying completely on her—simply because he had no
choice. It didn't alter the importance of her task. She
blinked hard a few times and began to write on the
first card, to her old nanny, now retired and living in
Bournemouth. Shelley and she had always kept in
touch. Nanny Hargreaves had been the one person she
could turn to in childhood, after her mother died.
With her father always away on business, there was no
one else...

She finished the card and looked up. The man had
gone. A flurry of brightly clad tourists came in talking
loudly. Americans, cheerful and laughing, brandishing
cameras—but of the man there was no sign. Shelley began to write on the other cards. When they were all
finished and safely despatched, she took the elevator
up to her room, opened the door with her key, and
went in.

The man who had been sitting by the open window

stood up, turned, and said in a deep pleasant voice:
'Good morning, Miss Regan, forgive my intrusion, but
I wish to speak to you.'

Her first instinct was for flight, and her hand was
already on the door handle, turning it, when he said:
'I know the real reason you have come to Avala, Miss
Regan—the secret reason—and we have much to talk
about.'

She hesitated, fear replaced by dread, and turned
slowly. Face ashen, she whispered: 'What do you
mean?'

He shrugged: 'Please believe me, I mean you no
harm. By all means have the door open if it makes you
feel safer, but you may like to consider that what I have
to say is very private.' He spoke English with a foreign
accent, and the high cheekbones seemed to betray
Slavik origins. He was dangerous, certainly—if he knew
why she was here, but she sensed no physical threat
from him. She relaxed her hold fractionally on the door
handle and looked at him.

'Who are you? And what do you mean, you know the
secret reason I'm here?'

'Forgive me. My name is Vargen Gilev and I am the
owner of this hotel, Miss Regan. My father was Russian,
my mother French.' He made a small, oddly formal
bow. It did not seem incongruous despite the fact that
he was dressed very casually in grey slacks and dark
blue short-sleeved shirt. He had an immense dignity
about him—yet also a ruthlessness, a hardness about his
face that belied his quiet words. And she could not
move away, because she had to listen to what he would
say. She had to find out if he did know the truth of her
visit. She waited, feeling cold, despite the tropical heat.
She waited for him to tell her.

'I know that you are here to buy the Hotel Catalina

at the other side of Avala. The auction is in two days.
You have come on the instructions of your father, because he does not want it known that he is to be the
buyer, and he has sent you, using a different surname
—because it is essential that the present owner of the
Hotel Catalina does not know who you really are.'

Shelley went over to her bed and sat down. The man
who was saying the dreadful, unbearable words sat
down again in the chair by the window. He was several
feet away from her. His face was shadowed, with the
sunlight behind him, but the force and power of his
personality filled the room. Shelley found that she was
trembling. 'Why are you telling me this?' she asked in
a barely audible voice.

'So that you will realise I know everything about
you.'

'So?' She stared at him, her natural self-confidence
returning. She was a fighter. She had had to learn
toughness over the years since childhood. It was either
that or be submerged by the force of her father's personality. This man and her father were two of a
kind ...

'I too want the Hotel Catalina.'

'It's a public auction. Anyone can bid.' She stood up.
'If that's all you've come to say, Mr—er—Gilev, I suggest you leave.' He stood up as well, and walked over to
her, very tall and overpowering, close to, but she stood
her ground. To show fear would give him an advantage,
and he already had too many.

He looked down at her and she saw the unusual
tawny gold eyes, flecked with black, saw the hard
planes of his face, smooth tanned skin, faint beard
shadow—saw the sheer animal strength of him, and
couldn't look away. 'But that is not all I came to say,
Miss Regan—or should I call you by your real name,

Miss Weldon? There is more, very much more.'

'Then tell me.' She too was tall, slimly built, with long blonde hair and fair skin, and her blue eyes were filled with the contempt she felt for him.

'I can outbid you for that hotel. I can do it quite easily—or I can see that you buy it, and thus satisfy your father. It is very important for you to succeed, is it not?'

'You know so much already, you should know that,' she responded icily. 'Is that why you followed me round? To find out more?'

'No. To see if you would go near the Hotel Catalina.'

'Well, I didn't, did I? So you wasted your morning. Nor do I intend to until the morning of the sale. Thank you for warning me of your intention to outbid me. Forewarned is forearmed——'

'I told you for a reason.' He smiled. 'Because I have a proposition for you. I can guarantee you buying the Hotel Catalina, if you agree to what I am going to ask you. If you don't agree, I promise you will fail.'

'Get *out*,' she said, through stiff lips. 'Get out of this room! I don't want to know your proposition——'

'I think you had better listen,' he said calmly. 'For instance, are you aware that a man sent by your father has followed you out here to check on your every move? That is why I approached you here instead of in the foyer.'

'Don't be ridiculous!' she snapped, then she saw what was on his face and faltered. It was an expression almost of pity.

'His name is Walter Grey, he is staying in room 304, two rooms along from you, and he is an employee of your father's at his London office. He actually flew out the day before you, has already telephoned your father to report your arrival, and was also following you this morning. I have a record of his call, and the number he called, in my office downstairs. He will be at the auction on Friday, watching your every move.'

'Why are you telling me this?' She was shattered by his words. She had thought her father trusted her, but clearly he didn't. It made her feel faint and sick.

'So that you can see how important my proposition is—how essential for you to listen. I shall leave you now, give you time to think over my words. But reflect on this, Miss Weldon—your father's shadow falls on you everywhere. If you meet anyone here, or speak to anyone other than hotel employees, your father will be told. I wonder why?'

Shelley knew, she knew only too well. Which was why she had felt so proud, so trusted, actually being able to leave England on her own for the first time in her life. Her father controlled all her relationships, subtly moved in on any he didn't approve of, and wrecked them. She had thought a new step had been reached with her coming here, but it hadn't. It was all just the same. She looked away, down at the floor, a sick humiliation washing over her.

'How can you be sure he's not watching you now?' she asked. 'Waiting for you to leave my room?'

'Because he is "detained" downstairs in the writing room waiting for what he thinks is an important call from England. There will be a mix-up on the line.' He smiled softly. 'As soon as I go down it will be discovered that the "call" isn't for him, but for an American tourist of similar name. I will see you later, Miss Weldon.' He walked past her towards the door.

'Wait,' she said. 'This proposition—what is it?'

He paused, turned slowly. 'I need a wife. It is essential for me to be married within seven days. Think about it. I am asking you to marry me, Miss Weldon. It will be strictly a business arrangement, and need only last for six months, after which it will be annulled. If you agree, the Hotel Catalina is yours. If you refuse then you might as well return to England tonight, because I promise you, you will not buy it.'

'You're mad,' she whispered, and went towards him, impelled by her own anger. 'Get out. Get out—now!'

He stood and faced her. 'I shall return after lunch, about two. *Au revoir.*' The door opened, then was closed softly after him. She was alone. Shelley went over to the bed and sat down, numb and shaken.

There were things to be done. Once the initial shock was over she began to think more clearly, her brain working fast. She opened the door and waited. After a few minutes quick hurrying footsteps passed along the corridor, and she ran to the door and looked out to see a grey-haired middle-aged man opening the door to room 304.

'Mr Grey?' she called. He paused, looked at her with something approaching alarm on his face, and she knew. In that moment, she knew.

'Yes?' he answered, a look of vague apprehension in his eyes.

'Why were you following me around this morning?' she demanded. She was standing by him now, and she looked at him scornfully.

'I'm sorry, you must be mistaken, Miss——'

'Come off it!' she snapped. 'I saw you. Now, before I call the manager you'd better tell me why. I don't like nasty little creeps like you!'

He swallowed. She felt almost sorry for him. He would, after all, have to explain why he had failed to

her father, and that was a fact deserving of pity. 'Look
—er—there's been some—er——' he stammered, and
she cut in:

'Hold on! I recognise you, don't I? Walter Grey—
you work for my father! Now there's a coincidence!
Would you care to tell me what you're doing in Avala
before I phone my father and ask *him*?'

He closed his eyes. He might have been praying, or
merely seeking inspiration. Whatever it was he was doing she now knew beyond all shadow of doubt that
Vargen Gilev had spoken the absolute truth.

'He sent me to keep an eye on you,' he said miser-
ably. 'Oh, Miss Weldon, don't, please—I'll do anything——'

'I want to know your full instructions, and then I'll
consider whether or not I'll tell him. I want the truth,
mind, the full truth. Come back to my room.' She
turned and he followed. Shelley indicated a chair and
sat in the one by the window. 'Fire away,' she said.

'Your father wanted you watched all the time you
were here,' he said quietly. He looked as shocked as she
herself had been only minutes before, but like her, he
was fast rallying his composure. 'He wanted me to make
sure you didn't get talking to any men—er—or anything——'

'You mean you're here to make sure I don't enjoy myself?' she enquired sharply. 'Is that it?'

He nodded. 'More or less.'

'And what, pray, were you going to do if you'd seen
me picking up a gorgeous man somewhere?'

'Telephone him immediately.'

'And?'

He shrugged. 'I don't know. He'd probably phone
you straight away. I'm only following orders, Miss

Weldon.' She felt a surge of cold fury, not at the man sitting near her, but at her father. Even at a distance he expected to control her life.

'You can go,' she said after a few moments. 'I won't tell him, on one condition. You stop following me about. Tell him what you like when you report. Tell him I'm sunbathing, or reading—and minding my own business. I suppose you're going to the auction on Friday?'

'Yes,' he nodded unhappily.

'And you'll be reporting back immediately to let him know if I've succeeded?'

'Yes.'

'Then you can do that. But until then, leave me alone. I'm an adult, Mr Grey. I'm twenty-three. Do you honestly think I like being watched like a child?'

'No. But it's my job—it's important to me, Miss Weldon. I couldn't refuse when asked. No one ever refuses your father——'

'How true! I know that better than anyone. Don't worry, you keep your part of the bargain and I'll keep mine.' She stood up and held out her hand. 'I keep my word, Mr Grey.'

He too stood up, relief shining on his face. 'Thank you, oh, thank you!'

'I'm going down for lunch now. I suggest you eat out.' She smiled. 'Goodbye, Mr Grey.'

He went out quickly, and she gave him a moment or two to reach his room, picked up her bag and went down in the elevator. The dining room looked out over the pool, which was crowded with guests swimming, splashing, or merely sunbathing and sipping cool drinks round the edges. Shelley ordered a salad, and when the waiter brought it said: 'Will you tell Mr Gilev that I'd like to see him as soon as possible, please?'

The waiter, a slim black youth, smiled, showing perfect teeth. 'Mr Gilev, madame?'

'Yes. He is the owner, isn't he?'

'*Si*, of course—but is there some complaint, madame?'

'No, everything is perfect.' She gave him a warm smile. 'Please ask him.'

'*Si*, madame, right away.' He darted off, and she saw a brief huddle in the corner by the kitchens with her waiter, the head waiter, and another man. Then after a few moments the head waiter, a stocky Italian, came over beaming ingratiatingly.

'Madame? You wish to see Mr Gilev?'

'That's right.'

'He is a very busy man, madame. May I help?'

'Just tell him that Miss Regan of room 302 is in the dining room and would like to see him. If he says no, then okay. But try, will you?' and she gave him a warm smile, which clearly confused him, for he bowed and walked away.

Shelley waited. She had come to a decision over the last shattering half hour, and the sooner she saw Vargen Gilev to tell him, the better. If she didn't, she might change her mind, and she didn't want to do that. Not now. She was at a turning point in her life. It was now or never.

She looked up when she heard the footsteps on the polished tile floor, and Vargen Gilev was walking towards her table. 'May I sit down, Miss Weldon?' he asked.

'Of course.' She waited until he had seated himself opposite her. 'I've told Mr Grey to stop following me about. In return, I won't tell my father I know about him.'

'Is that why you asked me to come here? To tell me that?'

'No. I want to know why you want to marry me.'

'It is a long story.' He looked at her very steadily and very seriously. 'Are you considering my proposition?'

'Yes, I am.' She looked back at him with equal steadiness. 'But I won't get mixed up in anything illegal.'

'I promise you it is not. It is purely for business reasons, nothing faintly illegal. I am a very law-abiding citizen, I promise you.'

'And if I marry you, I buy the Hotel Catalina?'

'Yes.'

'Which comes first—the wedding or the purchase?'

'The purchase.'

'How do you know I will keep my word? I may just leave, once I've got the deeds of the Hotel Catalina.'

'I will accept your promise to the bargain,' he answered.

'Really?' She began to laugh in disbelief.

'Plus, of course,' he added, 'the fact that I would make sure you didn't leave the island.' He gave her an apologetic smile, which didn't succeed in hiding that hard ruthlessness that was inherent. Shelley gave a little shiver. She believed *that*.

He turned away and lifted his arm, and a few moments later the Italian head waiter came over with an ice bucket containing a bottle of champagne.

'Thanks, Sergio,' said Vargen Gilev. 'And tell the reception desk I am not to be disturbed.'

'Yes, sir, of course.'

'Will you have a glass of champagne with me, Miss Weldon?'

'Please. You'd better start calling me Shelley.'

'Thank you. And please call me Vargen.' He lifted his glass. 'To us.'

She lifted her own glass in response. The whole situation was assuming a dreamlike, almost bizarre quality. 'When do you want to get married?' she asked.

'On Saturday.'

'And it is strictly a business arrangement? A marriage in name only?'

'Yes, it is.'

'How do I know you'll keep to that?' she asked.

'You have my word.' He regarded her steadily with those unusual tawny eyes. 'Are you a virgin?'

The question was a shock, and she felt herself go pink. 'I don't think that's any of your business!' she said breathlessly, angrily.

'True, it is not. Except that I can assure you that if you are you will be doubly safe. My tastes do not lie in deflowering maidens. I prefer my women to be experienced, and I do not think that you are.'

'You're very personal,' she said. 'And what makes you think——'

'That you are not experienced in sex?' He smiled faintly. 'There is an air of innocence about you that is very refreshing——'

'And you're obviously an old hand!' she snapped.

His mouth twitched. 'Why do you think I need a wife?'

'I don't know, I'm sure,' she retorted. 'You've lost me. Is it to prove you're a man?' She hoped the jibe would hurt, but if it hit home, it didn't show. His expression didn't change.

'I don't feel the necessity for that,' he answered, and the expression in his eyes as he looked at her sent a warmth coursing through her veins. Dear lord, she thought, I'll bet he doesn't! 'However, the man with whom I am very concerned to go into partnership in a business venture feels my present life style is not conducive to security, and if I am married he will feel much happier. In fact he has said as much. It's marriage —or no deal. The deal is extremely important to me— so, I get married.'

'Two things,' she managed to say, recovering fast from the stunning impact of his calm words. 'One— why not marry one of the many women I'm *sure* you know very well, and two—don't you think it's totally dishonest to do what you're doing? What will your business partner think in six months when the marriage is annulled?'

'You have a logical and perceptive mind,' he answered. 'I'll take your second question first. By the time that six months has passed my new partner will have realised the value of the partnership—I need the chance to prove it, that's all. As for your first,' he smiled, 'it is quite simple. Yes, I know many women, but not one who would be willing to have a marriage in name only—or be willing to finish it at the end of six months, you understand?'

'Oh, perfectly,' she murmured. 'You're clearly too irresistible for *words*—they'd not be able to say good- bye.' She gave him a sweet, cool smile and saw the flash of something disturbing to her in his eyes, quickly dis- pelled as he added:

'But there is another reason.'

'Good heavens! Is there?'

'It is you,' he said softly, and Shelley felt a shiver of apprehension touch her spine at the way he said it. 'You are ideal for my purpose. The man I wish to enter part- nership with is extremely old-fashioned in some ways, and you have—what is the word I need?' he frowned. 'Ah, yes, class. You have class, Shelley. And that is something that cannot be bought in a store.'

'And your women haven't?' She felt obscurely angry,

but not sure why except that it was as if she was in a
flesh market, being weighed up for form.

'Not like you, no.' He regarded her very levelly, his
eyes hard, seeming to bore into her very mind. 'But let
us talk about you, Shelley. You have your reasons for
this sudden decision to agree to my proposal. I wonder
what they are?'

She had no intention of telling him the truth. She
couldn't even admit that to herself. She met his hard
glance calmly. 'Your blackmail is totally irresistible—
even if I don't find *you* so, like all the other women you
know.'

'No, it is not that.' His eyes darkened, and she had
the awful feeling that he could read into her very mind.
'It is that you have thought about my words regarding
your follower, Mr Grey, and then found that I spoke
the truth—and that upset you more than anything else
your father has ever done.'

'I don't want to talk about it,' she said breathlessly,
urgently, and looked away, round the large dining
room. It was practically empty now, cool and shadowed
in contrast to the brightness of the pool outside. She
wanted to get away from Vargen Gilev, but where
would she run to get away from a man like him?

'No, I am aware of that,' he said softly, and filled her
glass again from the frosted champagne bottle. 'Please
have some more. I did not realise that I was so near the
truth.'

'You're not!' she snapped, and glared at him. 'Hadn't
we better discuss practical arrangements?'

'I shall take care of everything.' He looked at his
watch. 'Perhaps we can dine at eight tonight, and I
will give you all the details?'

'Very well. Will you excuse me now?' She needed to
be alone to think of the enormity of what she had

agreed to do. She stood up, and he did so as well.

'Of course. Until eight?' He watched her go. As Shelley left the dining room she looked back. He was lighting a cheroot, sitting at the table she had just left. He seemed to be smiling.

CHAPTER TWO

SHELLEY showered, dressed in a cool blue cotton kaftan, and lay on the bed to think about the shocks that had piled on more shocks since the morning. She still reeled from their impact, and felt exhausted, as though she had been running for miles. She had too many things to think about, but uppermost was the one truth he had voiced, the truth she had not wanted to know, deep in herself. Yet he had said it, and it could not be unsaid. His words echoed and re-echoed in her exhausted brain: '—and that upset you more than anything else your father has ever done——' More than anything else —as though he *knew* what her father was like. Perhaps he did; he seemed to know everything else.

In three days she would be a bride. She would be legally married, and her father's determination for her to marry Alec Masters, the son of his oldest, and possibly his only friend, would be finally thwarted. She neither liked nor disliked Alec; it was impossible to have strong feelings about a man who was as lacking in personality as a blancmange. The pressure had been increasing subtly of late—and what her father wanted, he always got. Or always had, until now. Until today, when, safely thousands of miles away from him, she had at last known the truth. She moved her head restlessly on the pillow and felt the dampness of the tears that came. Shelley, alone and sad, wept for the love she had never had, nor ever would—the love of her father. Then, she slept.

The discreet buzz of the telephone penetrated

through the layers of sleep until she reached out and picked up the receiver and mumbled a sleepy hello. She had no idea what time it was, or even, for a moment, where she was.

'Miss Regan? This is the desk clerk, madame. Mr Gilev presents his compliments and asks if you will join him in his apartment for a drink before dinner.'

It took a moment for what he was saying to register. 'What time is it?' she asked.

'It is six-thirty, madame. He wondered if seven o'clock would be convenient. Also it has been arranged for you to move into the Orange Suite this evening.'

'Seven? Yes—but I don't know where his apartment is.'

'If you will ring down when you are ready, we will send up someone to escort you there. Thank you, madame, goodbye.' The telephone went dead and she looked at the receiver before replacing it. Drinks before dinner with her husband-to-be—it made a mockery of the words. A cold-blooded arrangement with a ruthless man was not a marriage. She got up and went into her small bathroom to wash.

She should have known he would live in a penthouse apartment. From the huge picture window the view of the island was spectacular. Shelley stood, glass of white wine in her hand, and looked out over it, seeing the deepening purple velvet of the sky changing to black before her eyes. The lights twinkled on all over the town like scattered gold dust, and seemed to link with the various boats and yachts moored in the bay. Avala was a wealthy island, a tourist trap, a stopping-off must for cruise liners from all over the world, situated as it was in the Indian Ocean, largest of a group of some thousand or so islands, some too small to be

shown on even a large scale map. She stepped out on to
the balcony and the evening air was cool upon her face,
a balm, a soothing to her chaotic thoughts. Vargen's
voice came from the small kitchen of the apartment
where he was taking ice from the fridge for his vodka.

'This is where we shall live, Shelley. Is it to your
taste?'

'The view from here is beautiful, incredible.'

He came in bearing a tray of glasses and bottles and
a bowl of almonds. 'I mean the apartment.' He had
changed, and was wearing cream-coloured slacks and
matching shirt that made him look incredibly tanned
—and very handsome. Her heart missed a beat. She
knew, quite suddenly, why any one of his women would
not want to relinquish a hold on him, once gained,
and she looked away quickly, lest he read her mind,
and looked instead around the enormous living room.
Softly and subtly lit, it was a cool picture of modern
elegance, uncluttered yet elegant and luxurious.

Shelley was well used to the luxury that money can
buy, but this was something different. The underlying
colours were muted blues and greens, clean and cool.
A long settee stretched the length of the picture window, and in front of it was an onyx table upon which
he set down the tray. 'Please sit down,' he said.

She sank back into the cushioned softness of white
leather, and after a moment he too sat down—not near,
yet not far; near enough. Shelley felt a shiver at the
thought that he might touch her. She felt vulnerable,
insecure, and more alone than she had ever done in
her life.

He poured vodka into his glass and raised it to her.
'Your health, Shelley.' She raised her own in response,
and the words were a mockery, because he didn't care
about her one way or the other. She was a business asset,

no more, and he was a subtle revenge on her father. That was why she was here, and for no other reason. She drank the cold dry wine and put her glass down on the table. It wasn't too late. All she had to do was tell him she wasn't going through with it, with the madness, and walk out, that was all. Then she would return to her father and tell him why she had failed. He had never forgiven her for being born; he would certainly never forgive her for failure either. There was a bitter taste in her mouth and she said:

'I hope you don't mind me speaking frankly, but when our travesty of a marriage is over I hope you appreciate that I will not be welcome back in my father's house. He'll probably finish with me the moment he hears I'm——'

'Married?' he finished the word she had hesitated to say, swallowed his vodka and put the empty glass down. 'I have a contract ready for you to sign after our wedding. You will be adequately provided for, I promise you. Would you like to see it now?'

'No. Saturday will do.' She looked at him in the soft light. His face was shadowed, and outside the night had fallen, and the air was of a velvet softness, a perfect setting for lovers. It was so beautiful that it was like a pain in her heart. She ached with a longing she didn't fully understand, and made a little sound of anguish and looked away. He was like her father, emotionless, hard, cold. She knew then with an inner certainty that he had never loved any of his mistresses. But had he ever loved any woman? That was one question she could never—would never—ask.

'Are you cold?'

'No.' She could look at him again. The spell was broken with his question. I am cold and lost, she thought, but you would never understand that. 'It's quite warm. I'd like to go out for a walk later. Is it safe?'

'On Avala?' He smiled. 'Not for women walking alone at night. It is better not to. I will take you for a walk if you wish, though.'

'Oh, no thanks.' She must have said it too hastily, for he raised an amused eyebrow.

'You would be quite safe with me.'

'I didn't mean that. It doesn't matter.'

'But I insist.' What did it matter? She shrugged.

'Very well. Thank you.' There came a discreet tap on the door, a pause, and two waiters came in pushing a trolley, huge and heavily laden.

'I prefer to eat up here,' said Vargen. 'I hope you are agreeable?' He speaks as if I have a choice, she thought.

'Of course.' She wondered if Grey had made his evening report to her father. She herself was expected to telephone home every night as well. She looked at her watch, which showed precisely seven. The waiters were swiftly laying the table at the far end of the large room, by yet another picture window. One was lighting the candelabra while his companion set out the cutlery. They worked in silence.

'May I telephone?' she asked Vargen.

'But of course—I have a private line from which you may dial any number you like. It is in my bedroom.' He stood up and looked at her. 'Come.' He led her up three steps and into a large comfortable-looking room which contained a giant bed upon which was spread a white silk bedspread. Shelley said nothing, but her eyes stayed upon it in a kind of hypnotised fascination. He appeared not to notice, but indicated the telephone on a bedside table. 'And the bathroom leads off from here,' he indicated a mirrored door, 'if you wish to wash before we eat.'

'Thank you.' Shelley waited until he had gone out, closing the door behind him, then crossed the room and picked up the receiver. She didn't want to telephone her father, and she had no intention of telling him anything until after the wedding. He was quite capable of stopping the ceremony, even if it meant him flying out himself. And now that her mind was made up, nothing was going to change it. Her mouth was dry as she waited for the housekeeper to answer. She hoped that her voice wouldn't betray her inner turmoil. Her father was very astute.

But he wasn't in. The housekeeper, Mrs Redmond, answered, and said:

'Oh, he told me to tell you he'd be in late. He says can you ring him at midnight your time. He'll be home then. He's lunching out and then golfing with Mr Masters.'

'I'll do that. Tell him I called, will you? Goodbye, Mrs Redmond.' Shelley hung up, feeling a sense of relief. England was several hours behind Avala. It was quite logical that her father should be out—and golfing with her would-be father-in-law. Only he never would be, not now. She went steadily out and stood for a moment at the top of the three steps, surveying the room. Vargen waited for her, glass in hand, standing by the window. The waiters had gone.

'I thought that I would serve our meal,' he said. 'I hope that——'

'For God's sake stop asking me if I'm agreeable,' she burst out. 'You make it sound as though you *care* or something. Please don't insult my intelligence!' She swept down the steps, her long blue cotton skirt rustling slightly as she went, and as she walked towards him she saw the dark flash of anger that showed briefly on his face before he controlled it. She felt a prickle of fear, followed by satisfaction. Perhaps, after all, he wasn't entirely devoid of emotion. He stood there quite still, watching her approach, and she wasn't sure why she kept on walking towards him, except that it was as if she was drawn irresistibly to do so. Then she was facing him, her face pale, because she had suddenly gone dizzy, only she wasn't going to let him see that. 'You don't need to pretend anything when we're alone,' she said, and she felt breathless, but it was as though she couldn't stop.

'Common courtesy costs nothing. Are you unused to it?' he said, his voice very cool, very controlled.

'Is that what it is?' The room began to sway and blur, and she caught her breath—and he touched her arm to steady her.

'What's the matter?'

'I don't know——' He put his glass down, took her other arm, and stood before her. His hands were warm, very strong where they held her arms, and he was only inches away and she had to look up at him because he was so tall, and she saw what was in his eyes and wanted to move away, but it was impossible. 'I went dizzy——'

'You ate little at lunch. In a climate such as this it is important to eat regularly.'

'I'm beginning to realise that. Please let me go, I'm all right now.' She wasn't. At least the faintness had passed, but what had taken its place was slightly more disturbing. His nearness was like a potent force that reached out to entrap her. She sensed the power in his fingers and in his body, and she was alone with him, totally alone, and she had never met a man who could so affect her physically as he did, and even though she didn't like him at all because of everything he was, she

could no longer deny that she found him totally fascinating. She lifted her face and saw the darkness in his
eyes, and heard his breathing change, and she wanted
him to kiss her. With a little cry she tried to free herself. 'Please——' she whispered. Her heart was thudding so violently he surely must hear it, her whole body
was suffused with treacherous warmth, and a tingling
sensation. She knew with a deep sure feminine instinct
that he was as aware as she, that the potential explosive situation was not imagined. It seemed that he
made an almost visible effort to move. She heard his
deep breath, then:

'Of course.' His voice had gone harder, harsher, and
he released his hold on her, but it was as if he still held
her. Neither moved away. Held in an invisible web of
tension, neither moved. They stood there by the window, and Shelley could see their two bodies reflected in
the glass, he so tall, powerful, she fragile-seeming, slim
and delicate, and felt herself beginning to tremble.

'I'm—hungry,' she whispered.

He moved then. It was almost as if her words had released him. 'Of course.' He stood aside to let her pass,
and held her chair for her, and she thanked him, then,
quickly, before she could think about it too much,
said: 'I'm sorry I said what I did before.'

'You were not feeling well.' He seated himself opposite her at the table. 'I am aware what you think of me
—and you are quite right, I am undoubtedly all the
things that you think—but you will be treated with
courtesy by me, because that is also the way I am.' The
anger had gone, his face and voice fully controlled. The
tension of only moments ago, the incredibly taut
thread of tension that had reached out to touch and
hold them both, had gone—and yet not completely.

Despite his cool, even words, something of it lingered, like a faintest breath of air in the room, and it was around them, near them, not touching, but there.

Set on a plate in front of Shelley was a delicious-looking concoction of seafoods and avocado. 'Please eat,' he invited.

'It looks quite delicious,' she murmured.

'There is a white wine. Would you like some now?'

'Later.' She managed to smile. 'Food first, I think.'

'Very wise. And after we have eaten, a walk will do you good.'

'Yes, of course.' The conversation, the trite words, were on a shifting level, as if underlaid with what could not be said. Shelley ate, and watched him pour himself a glass of the sparkling clear wine. He had his back to the window, his silhouette dark against it. The stars twinkled distantly, timelessly, diamond bright chips in a black velvet sky. The candles flickered in a slight breeze, and their light softened his features and made their corner of the room a gentle shimmer of gold. Imperceptibly the tension was building up, and there was nothing she could do about it, because she was in a situation so totally new and alien that it was almost frightening.

She wanted him to make love to her. She looked down at her plate, steadily scooping up the last of the soft fleshy avocado as she knew finally what she should have known before, when they had stood by the window, and he had touched her, and she felt the pulse beating in her throat and wondered why the thought hadn't filled her with shame. She had never wanted any man to make love to her before. She didn't even like him, but she wanted him. She wondered how soon she could escape. It had to finish now, now—before it was too late, before she humiliated herself beyond recall.

'I'm sorry,' she said, 'I can't go through with it.' She looked up at him and waited, tremulous, for the blast of anger.

'With the marriage?'

'Yes. I can't——'

'I see.' He stood up. 'Would you prefer chicken or lamb?'

She stared at him. 'Didn't you hear me?'

'Yes, I heard you perfectly. Perhaps it is best if we talk after we have eaten.'

'I don't want any——'

'You must eat. If you prefer, we will talk while we eat.'

'I'll have anything.'

'Very well.' She watched him deftly serving the succulent slices of lamb, adding the fresh vegetables, handing her the plate. He waited until he had served himself, then spoke. 'And what will you tell your father?'

'The truth. I can't go through with this—this masquerade.' She tried to eat some of the food, was unable to do so, and put the fork down. 'I'm sorry, Vargen, truly sorry—I'll have to go home and face my father's anger, and that, believe me, is not something I relish. But it suddenly came to me, just now, how wrong it is to marry as we're planning to do. If I—ever marry —I want it to be because I love the man I marry.' She paused. He didn't look angry; his face was expressionless. He was listening politely as if she were talking about the weather. 'I shall leave here tomorrow.'

When she had finished speaking there was a silence. It grew and grew until she thought she wouldn't be able to bear it a second longer. She bit her lip to stop herself crying out, and he said: 'Thank you for telling me.'

'Aren't you very angry?'

He looked at her. 'No. Did you expect me to be?'

'Yes.' She had to put her hands on her knees to stop them from trembling.

'And now I will tell you something, Shelley. The Hotel Catalina is already mine. I bought it in a secret deal two weeks ago. But I shall sell it to your father, via you, at the price I paid for it.'

Shelley didn't believe what she was hearing. She heard the words well enough, but it seemed to her a very sick, cruel joke, and she turned and ran from the table, hand to her mouth, running towards the bathroom. She stumbled up the three steps, into his bedroom and across to his bathroom.

When she emerged several minutes later she was white-faced but composed. Vargen had said such an incredibly cruel thing to her that she knew she had made the right decision to leave. He was not only cold and ruthless, but mentally sick. He was standing at the foot of the three stairs, waiting for her. Icily controlled, but fighting for every vestige of it, and now dignified, she said:

'Please let me pass. I shall leave your hotel tonight. I can only say one thing—I utterly despise you.'

'Did you think I was joking? I meant it.'

She looked at him with hatred and contempt in her eyes. 'Meant *that*?'

'I do not make jokes like that. I admire your courage —and for that reason, and that reason only, I am releasing you from the "blackmail" threat I hold over you. Tomorrow morning, first thing, we will go to my solicitor's, and I shall transfer the deeds of the Hotel Catalina to you.'

He caught her as she fell, and carried her over to the long settee by the window. When she opened her eyes he was kneeling beside her bathing her forehead with a dampened towel. 'I'm sorry,' she whispered. 'You mean it, don't you?'

'Yes. You have my word.' He said it so simply, but with a calm dignity that made her want to cry out. His word. She knew at that moment that whatever else he might be, or do, or not do, his word was inviolate.

'I don't know what to say,' she murmured, and to her horror began to cry.

'Don't say anything.' She heard his voice only faintly through the heartrending release from tension. And more. The floodgates of the years had opened. Years of emotions held in check, of love rejected, of loveless luxury in a sterile, barren household, all were released in those few moments. She felt his arms go round her, and trembled.

'Why do you weep? Is that not what you wanted?' he said, and then she was free. With a last, shuddering gasp, she stopped weeping.

'Yes.' Her voice was shaky. 'But I can't let you——'

'It is as good as done, I have given my word. Now, dry your tears and finish your meal, or you won't have the strength to fly home.' He pulled her to her feet, brushed a tear from her cheek, and led her over to the table. Didn't he know what he had just done? And didn't he know what his nearness did to her?

'Now, eat,' he ordered.

Shelley ate. When she had finished the meal she smiled. 'I feel much better,' she admitted.

'Good. Now go and sit by the window, and I will make coffee for us.'

She walked over to the window and sat down. Now, at last, the meaning of what he was prepared to do was sinking in. She could fly home tomorrow if she wanted, with the deeds of the Hotel Catalina in her handbag.

Mission accomplished, and her father pleased with her. And that, after all, was all she really wanted in life. She saw her father's face, smiling, and then in her mind's eye she saw Vargen, and knew that it wasn't enough at all. And when a few minutes later he came in carrying two cups and saucers, she looked up at him and said very quietly:

'My part of the bargain still stands. On Saturday I will marry you. You have my word on that.' She was fully composed, and she knew exactly why she was saying what she was. He didn't, and never would.

He sat down. 'Thank you.'

She took a deep breath. 'After we've drunk this coffee, can we go for that walk? We have a lot to talk about.'

'Of course,' he nodded. 'Whenever you are ready.'

They walked past the old harbour where the fishing boats bobbed gently on a calm sea, past the beach huts where fishermen lived with their families, and Shelley thought, I'll be living on this island for the next six months; it will be my home. It was a strange thought to have. I'll be living with him, but not living with him—and that was an even stranger thought to have. The arrangements were quite clear, cut and dried. Vargen had outlined them to her as they left the hotel, and he had talked and she had listened, and agreed, and accepted the terms of the mock marriage, because that was the way it had to be. She would be free to do as she wished, within reason, as long as she was prepared to act as hostess for his business friends, and for his godfather in particular—the man with whom, now, he would be in partnership. She was going to meet him for the first time at the wedding. The honeymoon would be spent cruising on Vargen's yacht. For six months Shelley would act the part of a loving bride, and then they would part. There would be a discreet annulment.

His words were clipped and precise. There was no tension, no shimmering threads reaching out to touch them both, any more. Vargen's mind was on business, and with him, as with her father, it was all-important. More important than anything. Why then, she wondered, had he made that quixotic gesture? She would never know. She had been free for a few moments, and she had thrown that freedom away. And the payment was just beginning.

They reached the end of a shingly beach track, which petered out into the sea, and there was a low wall covered in sand and shells. Vargen brushed some aside. 'We will sit here for a few moments and then return home,' he said.

Shelley sat down. The question that had been at the very back of her mind, nagging away at her, was ready to be asked. Let him be angry if he chose—she had to know. 'Will you be seeing any of your—female friends —after we're married?' she asked, and the words didn't come easily.

He sat beside her and she moved fractionally away without being aware of it. 'I do not possess the constitution of a monk,' he answered. 'Does that answer your question?'

It did, but she couldn't let it go at that. 'No,' she said, 'it doesn't. Will you?'

'Yes. But I shall be discreet.'

Her heart thudded. She wanted to hurt him, unaware that the sickening pain that filled her was jealousy. She had never loved any man enough to be jealous. 'Discreet?' she echoed. 'How will you manage *that* on an island this size?' She tried to keep her voice calm, but she was finding that difficult.

'There are many islands near here, and I have a boat,' he said. 'Is this something we need to discuss?'

'Yes, it is,' she retorted. 'I'm entitled to know. I suppose you've got a few mistresses tucked away on various islands—is that it?'

'Only one at the moment.' He looked at her tight face. 'And I'm not going to tell you her name, so you needn't ask me.'

'And does she know that you're getting married on Saturday?'

'How could she? I didn't know myself until today.'

'She'll accept it?'

He shrugged. 'When she knows——'

'You'd tell her the real reason?'

'It is only fair——' he began.

'Fair?' She felt her voice rising and tried desperately to control it. 'Fair? And if she tells your godfather——'

'Why should she? She is well treated for her services.'

She caught him a stinging slap on his cheek, lashing out impulsively, torn by such an intensity of emotion that it frightened her. She heard him catch his breath sharply and she sat there, her breast heaving, her body shaking with anger. Then he simply turned and walked away from her. She watched him go, and she couldn't have moved away at that moment if she had wanted to.

The line of trees along the edge of the beach now hid him, and she was alone. She didn't care. He had left her, and it didn't matter. Nothing mattered any more. She pictured herself lying in bed, hearing him go out —and waiting for him to return from the arms of his mistress, and she wondered if she would be able to bear it.

There was no sound save the shush of the water over the sand. She was alone, as she had always been all her life, and always would be. She jumped off the wall and set off walking back along the beach towards the shingle track. Then a shape moved, a dark shadow of a man walking outward from the blackness of the trees, and she tensed, then saw that it was Vargen.

'I thought you'd gone,' she said.

'I would not have left you alone here. Did you think I would? I was waiting for you here.'

'I'm sorry I hit you,' she said quietly.

'Why did you do it? I was answering your questions, that is all.'

'I don't know. You sounded so cold-blooded, somehow.'

'Perhaps because I am, Shelley. As you will no doubt learn.'

'Do you love this woman?'

'No.'

'Have you ever loved a woman?'

He stopped walking and looked down at her. 'Why do you ask?'

It had been the forbidden question, the one she had intended to remain unspoken, and she didn't know why she had asked, any more than he did. Except that it was more of the sweet, agonising torture for her. 'I wanted to know,' she whispered.

'Yes, I have. Very much. I loved a woman once, so much that I would have given her my life if she had asked. But she didn't love me—as I found out one day in the most painful way possible. And since then, no, I have not loved any woman. Nor will I ever. Does that answer your question, or would you like to see me bleed?' She saw the dark pain in his eyes, and was silenced. Shattered, she looked at him, and then, because it was unbearable, looked away and whispered:

'I'm sorry.'

'Don't be. I'm not. I learned the lesson well.' He caught hold of her chin and forced her to look up at him. 'I use women now. I satisfy my needs, and that is the end of it. Am I being blunt enough or do you want to hear more?'

'No, that's enough. You've said enough. Please, you're hurting me, Vargen!'

He released her abruptly and turned away. He seemed to be fighting for control and she saw the tension in his arms as his hands clenched, and for a dreadful instant she thought he would strike her, and she waited, tense and frightened, unable to move. He turned back and she flinched, took a step backward, and said: 'Don't——'

He frowned. 'What?' He seemed to have been a long way away.

'I thought you were going to hit me——' She was poised, ready to run; useless, she knew, but that was better than standing there, and she heard him sigh.

'Did you think *that*?' he asked.

'Weren't you?'

'No! How could I?'

'You looked as if——'

'*Hit* you? What kind of man do you think I am?' For the first time Vargen sounded angry. He stared down at her, eyes dark and shadowed. 'Do you think I could be capable of striking a woman?'

'I don't know you, do I?' she said. 'We're strangers. You were angry——'

'I have never touched any woman in anger in my life. Yes, we are strangers, and may always be so, but I will never hit you. It would be impossible for me to do so. Has any man ever struck you? Is this why you were frightened? Tell me.'

There was a long, dreadful pause, then: 'Only—my father——'

'*Chort!* When? When you were a child?'

'Yes—but I particularly remember the time when I was fifteen. He caught me talking to the gardener's son —my age—in the gardens. We weren't doing anything, just talking, but it was dark—and he took me back into the house and——' she had to swallow. The memories were painful to remember. 'He beat me with his riding whip.'

Vargen put his hand to his forehead. She saw his face contort—for only an instant, but that was long enough —into a dreadful anger. Then it was gone. 'We had better go back now,' he said. 'I have never heard anything so appalling.'

'I got over it,' she answered. 'It was the gardener I felt most badly about. My father sacked him the following day. I felt dreadful for ages, but there was nothing I could do about it.'

'No. I should not have asked,' he said. 'Come, it is late, and we have much work to do tomorrow.'

They set off walking. But now there were no more questions. They walked in silence back along the path, through the town, and towards the hotel. It was brightly lit, and people wandered in and out as though it were daytime. Shelley wondered what Walter Grey was doing, then remembered that she had to telephone her father.

Vargen took her up in the lift to a higher floor, immediately below the penthouse. It wasn't until he opened a different door for her that she remembered the desk clerk saying she would be moved. She went in and looked around the sumptuous living room of a suite, then at Vargen. 'Is this *mine*?'

'Yes. All your possessions are here.' He handed her a key.

'Is there a phone? My father wasn't in before.'

'You are going to telephone now?'

'Yes. Is it all right?'

'Of course. Shelley, I would like to speak to him. May I?'

Alarm flared. 'No! That's impossible——'

'Please.'

'But why?'

'To tell him that we are going to be married.'

CHAPTER THREE

'To *tell* him? Are you mad?' she gasped.

'No, very sane. It is right that he should know, surely?'

Shelley took a deep breath. 'I'll tell him myself, after the wedding.'

Vargen nodded. 'Very well, if that is how you wish it.' His face was hard and cold, and she thought suddenly, I don't know him at all. I never will, yet in a few days we'll be on our honeymoon. She was still shaken after what had happened on the beach, one event following another in a confused tumble of emotional turmoil that had left her shattered. He was a man of deep dark emotions, a man of anger and passion—a man who had once been hurt in a way that had changed his life, and in a matter of hours he would put a wedding ring on her finger to finalise an arrangement that she had agreed to because of so many complicated factors that she was no longer sure herself exactly what they were. But her father must not know until it was too late. That seemed most important of all.

Shelley felt very tired all of a sudden. She sat down in a chair, and Vargen asked: 'Would you like a drink?'

She shook her head. 'I don't think so, thanks.'

'You have your own small kitchen, with a refrigerator. There is a selection of drinks, and a tray of ice cubes.'

'Is there?' She looked up at him, then around the room. 'It's very kind of you, but it wasn't necessary to have me transferred here, you know.'

He shrugged. 'It is only for a day or so. After our marriage we will live in the penthouse suite.'

'Yes. I think—I'll have a drink, please.' She felt stifled. She didn't want to think about that—yet. Time enough when the knot was tied. Vargen walked out of the room and she looked across at her reflection in a long wall mirror. She looked pale and tired, her smooth honey-gold hair framing her face softly in the warm light from the two lamps he had switched on. She was slim, and seemingly fragile, and the low-necked cotton lace blouse that she wore emphasised the delicacy of her features, and the faint smudges of tired-ness beneath her eyes made them seem larger. She regarded her reflection dispassionately for a few moments until he returned carrying two glasses, and handed her one. His back was reflected in the mirror. He was straight and tall, and when he walked it was with an unconscious grace of movement that emphasised his steely strength. He was a powerful man, and he was ruthless, she knew that already, but he also possessed a veneer of charm that could make her forget briefly what she was getting into.

'It is a white, rather dry wine,' he remarked, as she began to sip it. He sat down in a nearby chair and regarded her coolly over his glass. 'Tomorrow you will choose your wedding dress. I will arrange for a car to come when you are ready.'

'I see. Is all your business so well organised?'

'Yes.' The tawny eyes seemed to hold a flicker of amusement, but it might have been her imagination. 'I may also have some rings ready for you to try on to-morrow.'

A pulse beat in her throat as she looked at him. The conversation was bizarre, but no more so than anything else that had happened. He might have been discussing the price of stocks and shares, it was as impersonal as that.

'Is the whole farce necessary?' she asked. 'Why not just pretend to be married?'

'On an island this size?' he smiled slightly. 'Impossible.'

'I see.' She finished the wine, which left her feeling pleasantly muzzy. 'And in any case, it's better for your "women" to know, isn't it? Hadn't you better arrange for a photographer as well?'

'That will also be done.'

'Of course,' she agreed smoothly. 'I should have known.' She looked at her watch. 'I'm tired, Vargen. If you don't mind——'

He rose to his feet. 'Naturally. Until the morning, then. Telephone me if there is anything you need. I have given instructions to the reception that you are to be put through to me at any time you call. Goodnight, Shelley.' He put his glass down on the table, and she stood up as well. As he walked towards the hallway of her suite she followed, not sure why, except that it seemed important to her to make sure he went. He turned, almost at the outer door, so that she nearly collided with him, and he looked down at her.

Instantly, within that split second of time, tension filled the small hallway. Shelley caught her breath, her heart thudding. For a moment she wondered if he was going to touch her. He was only inches away, warm and vital, and she could feel the tension flowing round them, and knew that he was aware of it as well as her.

'What——' she began, breathless, afraid, not knowing why, heart hammering.

He opened his mouth as if to speak, hesitated, then as if almost visibly controlling himself said: 'I would

like you to meet my godfather tomorrow. Would it be
agreeable for you to have dinner in my apartment with
him and his wife?'

'Of course.' But she wondered if that had been what
he had intended saying; it seemed to her——

'He and his wife are staying on the island. They have
a villa here. When you go for your dress tomorrow, will
you also buy some clothes for evening wear, and the
honeymoon?'

'Some.' She shook her head. 'The allowance doesn't
cover all I'd need——'

'All you buy will go on to my account. Did you think
I expected you to pay?'

She hadn't thought about it. She looked at him. The
tension was there, almost tangible, a shimmering cloak
surrounding them. She wanted to lash out, she didn't
know why. She wanted to hurt him. 'I'd forgotten that
you'd bought me,' she said.

She heard the slight hiss of his swiftly indrawn
breath. Then: 'I haven't. But we have a business
arrangement, remember?'

'How could I forget?'

'I shall go now—before you lose your precarious
temper again,' he answered swiftly, smoothly, and she
retorted:

'Yes, perhaps you'd better. Put it down to pre-
wedding nerves.' Her nerves *were* ragged, and she
wanted to cry. 'Although I'm sure they won't affect you.'

'Nothing affects me. Remember that.' It seemed almost like a warning. She took a step back.

'Please go.'

'Goodnight, Shelley.' He opened the door and went
out. She closed it after him and collapsed against it,
breathless as though she had been running. She stood

there for a few moments, seeing his face clearly in her mind's eye, and shivered. After a few seconds she went to telephone her father.

Shelley chose a simple white silk dress for her wedding. Floor-length and slim-fitting, with a low scooped-out neck and long loose sleeves, it made her look very young and innocent. She looked at herself in the mirror, and the two girl assistants who had been deputed to look after her stood back and gasped in admiration. Native Avalans, honey-skinned and dark-eyed, both were young, cheerful and pleasant.

'It is beautiful,' whispered the senior girl. 'It is perfect for you, madame.' Shelley knew they weren't saying it in hopes of making a sale. The girl meant it— and Shelley knew why. It might have been made for her.

'Yes,' she said softly, 'this is the one.' She smiled at them. They didn't know the truth, of course. This shop belonged to Vargen, and quite clearly they had their instructions to cater to her every whim. It was also equally clear that they considered her a very lucky woman. She had been ushered in by both of them when the chauffeur had dropped her at the store, and had been shown a dazzling array of clothes to suit every occasion. This, now, the wedding dress, was the culmination of three hours' shopping. She was on the second floor of the large building, and it had become apparent that other customers were being kept away from this section, for the only people she had seen in those three hours were her two assistants and a junior who had been kept busy running up to the stockroom for more dresses. A glass jug filled with fresh pineapple juice was on a nearby table. Shelley went over to pour herself a drink, and the melting ice clinked coolly in the glass.

'Do help yourselves,' she said. 'This must be thirsty work for you.'

The junior was despatched for glasses and more fruit juice, and Shelley took the dress off and sank back into a chair. She wore only a cool cotton slip and briefs.

'Madame,' said Pelma, the senior of the two girls, with some hesitation, 'Mr Gilev has instructed us to deliver the clothes to the hotel today. But if you wish us to help you on Saturday, we will both be delighted.' The other girl, Rose, nodded, smiling broadly.

'That's very kind of you,' Shelley answered. 'Do sit down a minute.' The harassed junior deposited fresh drinks and glasses down and scooted away, and Pelma and Rose sat down obediently. If I told them to stand on their heads in the corner they'd probably do that as well, thought Shelley. She was feeling weary of the whole sham affair. 'I'd appreciate help.'

'I'm a hairdresser,' Rose volunteered. Her dusky face creased in a huge smile. 'Would you like me to do your hair?'

'Yes, please, I would.' She looked at the discarded dress. 'Something simple, I think.'

'Madame's hair is beautiful as it is, but perhaps a soft wave?'

'I'll leave it to you.' Shelley leaned back and closed her eyes. 'If you can be at the hotel at eleven, perhaps? The wedding's at one.'

'Of course. May we say——' Pelma hesitated slightly, 'how happy we hope you'll be? Mr Gilev is—we all think a great deal of him——' She lowered her eyes as if she had been impertinent, and Shelley saw her bite her lip.

Not you as well! she thought wryly. 'Thank you,' she answered, then looked at her watch. She wanted to get away. One more day before her wedding, and she wanted to escape before it was too late. She wanted to be alone to think. 'Will you arrange to have everything delivered? I'm going to walk back to the hotel.'

'But the car—we were told to ring for it to take you back when you had finished here——'

'No, I just want to take a walk, that's all.' She stood up and slipped her cool white cotton dress over her head. 'Thank you both for all your help. I'll see you about eleven on Saturday.' A quick flick with a comb through her hair and she was ready. She saw their anxious looks at each other as she left them, and it was like all the times before, with her father, the watching, the feeling of never being entirely free. In six months I will be, she thought, as she walked down the wide staircase, and out of the store.

She had forgotten just how hot it would be. The store's air-conditioning was superb, which only made the blast of air that hit her more powerful in contrast. She tried to take a few deep breaths, and began walking slowly through the crowds of tourists and natives to and from the noisy, busy market nearby. She put on her sunglasses, and now she was truly alone, and free to think. No one to bother her, for no one knew who she was. Her shadow, Walter Grey, would be waiting at the hotel, probably biting his nails and wondering about the auction tomorrow. She felt quite sorry for him. She would warn him later ... It didn't seem very important at the moment, nothing did. Tonight she would be having dinner with Vargen's future business partner, and that would be the real start of the deception.

In the bay, swimmers splashed about in the cool-looking green water, and she paused at the top of the slope leading down towards the beach and watched

them. The shark nets were well marked with buoys,
and the swimmers kept within their limits. The sun
beat down from an almost white sky, and from somewhere behind her a car's horn blared in the traffic, and
the hotels and shops lining the promenade shimmered
and dazzled in the sunlight. Practically every building
was white. Only the market provided a splash of colour
with the many stalls selling multi-hued rugs and stoles
and lengths of materials for the tourists to take home.
Voices hummed around her, eddying and swirling in
waves of sound. She wondered if any of the tourists had
lives as complicated as hers. There was laughter, and
there was music from a strolling hippy guitar player,
and the heat beat up from the grey stone beneath her
feet and she felt very tired. But she wasn't going back
yet. Not yet. She sat down on a flat rock and gazed out
to the distant horizon.

A cruise liner moved gracefully towards Avala from
the distance. One was already moored some way out,
and boats were ferrying passengers ashore to where
pony traps waited a mile or so away. Shelley lifted her
face towards the sun, drinking in the blazing heat,
closing her eyes behind the all-concealing sunglasses.
And she began to think of her uncle.

It was past lunchtime, but she didn't feel hungry,
only thirsty. She felt immensely sad. Then, gradually,
something changed. Now was the opportunity to alter
her life, and she wasn't going to spoil it with doubts
and regrets. Nothing could be worse than life with her
father, and his moods and his anger. She had accepted
the chance to alter it irrevocably. She would be free of
him on Saturday, free for ever. She got up and began
to walk purposefully towards her uncle's hotel, the one
she had come to buy secretly. In a way, it was already

hers. Two days ago she would not have dreamed of going there. Her father's instructions had been very precise on that point, but now they weren't important. She had been very fond of Uncle Victor, as a child, before the quarrel and the silence. It wasn't too late to make it up.

The hotel was further along the front, in a prime position, a large white building surrounded by palm trees and bright flowering bushes. A wide crazy paving drive led up to the main entrance. Shelley entered the cool foyer, waited a moment for her eyes to adjust to the darker interior, then went over to the desk.

'Is Mr Weldon here, please?' she asked the reception clerk, a young man.

He looked smilingly but warily at her. 'Mr Weldon, madame? I will see. Who shall I say is wanting him?'

'I'm his niece, Shelley Weldon.'

'One moment, please.' He turned away, picked up a telephone, spoke quietly, low-voiced, while she waited.

Then he turned to her. His voice more deferential, he said: 'Please, this way, Miss Weldon.'

She was ushered along a corridor to a room at the end, the young man gave a discreet tap on the door, and it opened and her uncle stood there, a look of stunned disbelief on his face.

'Shelley,' he began. 'Oh, Shelley——' his voice broke, then she was in his arms and he was hugging her delightedly, laughing and crying all at the same time. 'My God, by all that's wonderful!' Victor Weldon stepped back, still keeping hold of her hands. 'Let me look at you. My, you've grown up! What on earth are you doing here, my dear?'

He was tall and more broadly built than his brother, and at fifty-seven he was eight years older than Charles

Weldon, but his eyes were kinder, and in that split second as they looked at each other Shelley felt a surge of regret for all the wasted years.

'It's a long story,' she said. 'If you've got time to listen?'

'How can you even ask? Sit down, sit down.' He waved apologetically round at the paper-strewn desk. 'Don't mind the mess. I've a lot of work on sorting this out.'

She sat down. 'I think I know why,' she said softly, 'and in a way, it's why I came here to Avala.'

He pulled a chair near to her and sat down. Puzzled, but still smiling his pleasure at seeing her, he said: 'Did you know I'd sold this place?'

'Yes,' she nodded. 'I'd better begin at the beginning.' She smiled at him, remembering how kind he had always been to her as a child. She should have come before now...

The story took time to tell, and he listened intently, his expression growing more stunned as her words tumbled out. When she had finished he stood up.

'My God!' he whispered. 'Shelley, I can't believe all this!'

'It's true, every word,' she said. Tears shone in her eyes. 'Oh, Uncle Victor, I had to come and tell you. I should have come ages ago.'

He sat down again and took her hand. 'My dear child, I just don't know what to say. You're marrying Vargen Gilev on Saturday—it's just—unbelievable!'

'Yes, I know it is, but it happens to be true.' Her eyes were very bright with the unshed tears. 'It's a business arrangement——'

'I can't let you!'

She shook her head. 'It's all right, I've been over everything in my mind already.'

'But you don't know him!'

'Do you?' she asked quietly.

'Yes, Everyone does.'

'Well? He's not a monster, is he?'

'No!' he smote his forehead. 'It's not that! He's hard—he's all steel. He's the toughest man I've ever met in my life. Compared to him, your father's a babe in arms. I can't let you—I'll phone him now——'

'He owns this hotel,' she cut in.

'Damn that! Do you think I care if Charles doesn't get his own way for once? You're very precious to me—it's you I'm thinking about, my dear. I can't let you walk into any kind of marriage with a man like Vargen Gilev. He'll break your heart!'

'He won't. Don't you see? I'll be free——'

'You can be free now. Stay here. I was planning to stay on as manager for a while—obviously before Gilev met you and thought up this mad scheme. You can stay with me, whether here, or not. I've got money——'

'It's not that. I've given him my word,' she said quietly.

He looked at her, saw what was in her face and was silenced for a moment. Then: 'My dear, I admire your courage,' he said quietly. 'But I'm still going to phone him.'

She shrugged. 'All right, but it won't make any difference. Uncle may I have a drink? Something nice and cold.'

'Of course. Do forgive me.' He pressed a button on the telephone, picked it up, and when it was answered asked for drinks to be brought in, and also for an outside line. Shelley waited with a sense of calm finality. It was rather pleasant, having someone who cared about her as a person. She watched him dial, and during the time he was waiting to be put through to Vargen a waiter brought in a tray of drinks and left them.

'Gilev? Victor Weldon here. Shelley's with me——'
there was a pause while her uncle listened, then: 'I see.
Yes, I'd like to meet you too. Say, ten minutes? Goodbye.' He put the receiver down, his face thoughtful.
'One gets the impression he's not too pleased at you
being here. Did he not know?'

'No. I was buying clothes, and afterwards, instead of
taking his car back to the hotel, I set off for a walk.'

'I see.' He smiled warmly at her. 'I'm so glad you did.
But you don't seem to have pleased him overmuch. I
told you he was hard, didn't I?'

'I already know that. And I've lived with my father
all my life, remember? I'm used to it by now.'

'No, not *his* kind of ruthlessness, you're not. He's one
on his own, is Vargen Gilev. Truly he is.'

'Don't you like him?'

Her uncle laughed, startled. 'Funnily enough, I do.
Or did.'

'Then why like him if he's as hard as you say?'

'Because he also possesses a tremendous charm—a
charisma. He's also straight. He bought this place at a
fair price. And his word is as sound as a bell, but——'

'No buts. Let's wait until he arrives, shall we?'

He shrugged. 'Here, drink some more orange juice.
You're right, let's wait.'

They didn't have long. There was a knock at the
door and Shelley's future husband walked in. Instantly
the atmosphere was charged, as though with electric
currents. Shelley saw Victor's face in the second before
the two men shook hands. He was as tense as a coiled
spring.

'Hello, Victor,' said Vargen, then turned to Shelley.
'I did not know where you were, Shelley. Had you let

me know I would have arranged transport.' His tone was mild as if he were unaware of the atmosphere.

'I wanted to be alone for a while to think,' she said, looking at him. 'Then I decided to visit my uncle.' Her eyes were cool and calm on him. He *was* aware of the tension, because he was creating it, and she was letting him know that she didn't care. His eyes returned the glance with equal coolness, and they were as hard as she had ever seen them.

'Shelley,' said her uncle, 'I'd like to speak to Vargen alone.'

'No,' she answered, 'I'm staying.'

'She has told you of our arrangements?' asked Vargen, looking at her uncle.

'Yes. I don't like anything about this——'

'That is only what I expected, Victor. I'm sorry I couldn't tell you myself, I think you would have seen it differently.'

'There's nothing to see differently, is there?' Victor Weldon looked at the taller, younger man, and Shelley felt an instinctive rush of affection for him. He cared for her, he cared deeply, and the thought warmed her.

'You are marrying Shelley for a purely selfish motive. She is my niece and I love her dearly—and I don't want this to happen.'

'I accept your viewpoint. But do you not think Shelley is mature enough to decide for herself?'

'No, I don't.' Victor walked nearer to Vargen. 'Because of the life she has led, I don't. She sees you as a chance for escape from her father's domination—and it's the wrong way to do it. She can stay here if she wants.'

Vargen turned slowly to Shelley. 'Is that what you want, Shelley?'

'No. I've given you my word,' she said quietly. She looked at her uncle. 'Thank you for caring, but it's too late.'

'It isn't,' he said harshly.

She stood up and went over to hug him. 'It is,' she whispered. 'And I know what I'm doing, believe me.' He held her tightly and looked over at the waiting man.

Vargen watched them both, then he spoke. He spoke as if he had considered the words carefully first. 'Shelley, please let me speak to your uncle alone.'

She pulled away from her uncle, looked at Vargen, saw his eyes, and took a deep breath. 'All right,' she said. She walked to the door and Vargen opened it for her.

'We will not be long,' he said quietly.

'I'll be in the foyer.' She walked out with head held high. She had no idea what they were going to say, but she had no desire to stay. In a way it had gone beyond her. She felt as if she were in a kind of dream state as she walked back into the foyer, found a cool seat in a corner, picked up a magazine, and prepared to wait.

The young receptionist appeared at her side. 'May I get you a drink, madame?' he asked.

'Please, Bacardi and Coke.'

'At once, madame,' he said, and vanished. She was left to her thoughts. What were they saying? She felt as if she might float away at any moment.

The young man returned with the drink, and she sipped it, then looked up at the sound of a distant door closing, to see both Vargen and her uncle approaching.

She put the glass on the table and stood up as the two men stopped before her. Her uncle seemed less tense. Vargen seemed exactly the same.

'I'm coming to dinner this evening,' said her uncle. 'We mustn't lose touch now—not ever again.'

'We won't.' She kissed him, and Vargen said:

'The car is waiting outside. Shall we go?' He turned to Victor and they shook hands. 'Until seven, then?'

'Yes. Seven.'

They walked out into the furnace, Vargen's car rolled silently up and they got in. Shelley looked back. Her uncle stood on the steps, waving. She leaned back and closed her eyes for a moment. 'What did you say to him?' she asked. Vargen leaned forward to close the glass partition between them and the driver.

'We talked business,' he answered.

'Really? Do you ever talk about anything else?'

'Yes, sometimes.'

'Were you angry because I'd left the shop without telling you where I was going?'

'No. Should I have been?'

'My uncle said you didn't sound very pleased when he phoned.'

'I was not pleased. It would have been good manners to have told me you wished to walk alone. But I wasn't angry. I am rarely angry.'

'I forgot,' she answered.

'Forgot what?'

'You have to be human to get angry, to have emotions. You don't have any, do you?'

'No.'

The subject was closed. He turned away, and the rest of the ride was accomplished in silence. When they reached their hotel he dismissed the driver and they walked in. 'I'm going to swim in the pool,' Shelley told him. 'If you don't mind.'

He shrugged. 'But of course. Remember that your uncle is coming at seven.'

'I will.' He pressed the elevator button and the doors slid open. When they reached her floor he got out of the elevator with her and walked along the corridor.

'I'm going to change,' she told him.

'I wish to speak to you first,' he answered, took her key from her and opened the door. Inside the suite it was cool, the windows closed, the air even slightly chilly. He followed her into the sitting room and she put her bag down and turned to him.

'What do you want to say?' she asked.

He stood there looking at her. Dressed very simply in cream pants and matching shirt, open-necked, short-sleeved, he was tall, attractive, and very powerful-looking.

'Your uncle was concerned about our marriage,' he said. 'Not simply because it is an arrangement he finds very cold-blooded—I use his words—but because he thought that I, being the man I am, would be unable to keep my promise of it being a marriage in name only.'

'That's natural enough,' she remarked. 'Is that all you wanted to say?'

'Not quite. Does it worry you as well?'

'We've been over this already, haven't we?' she said. 'You gave me your word. That's enough.'

'Yes, it would be—only——' he hesitated. Vargen, hesitating? Surely he wasn't lost for words? She gazed at him, surprised at the change in his expression.

'Only?' she prompted.

'He knew something you do not. And perhaps it is better you hear it from me instead of from him.'

Shelley sat down very slowly. She had the strangest feeling that she was going to hear something of great significance. She couldn't imagine what it could be, for what more could there be to tell? And yet his face held a knowledge she found disturbing. Her breath caught in her throat.

'Tell me,' she whispered.

'Your uncle is aware that—I know—your father,' he said.

She went dizzy. 'I—don't understand.' Her voice was very faint.

'No, you wouldn't. But five years ago, when I was in Paris visiting my godfather, and on a business trip, I met him.'

She looked up, eyes wide, vulnerable, afraid. 'And?' she whispered.

'He was on the—shall we say—opposing side in the business deal.'

'Please, I'd rather not hear any more,' she said. She could hardly get the words out. 'I don't want to know——'

'Perhaps you must. It will explain your uncle's distress when you told him that we were marrying. Because he thinks I want revenge on your father, because of what happened in Paris.'

'Do you?' She looked up. 'Is that why——'

'No.' His voice was harsher, deeper. He turned away and walked towards the window. 'Your father is no longer part of it. But Victor doesn't understand that. He thinks, because I knew you were coming here——'

This was worse than anything that had gone before. He had known—had *known*—— Ashen faced, she jerked back.

'You knew I was coming? You *knew*?'

'Yes.'

'H-how—did—you——' She clutched the sides of the chair to steady herself.

'How did I know?' He gave an odd little smile. 'I know everything about your father. I have made it my business to do so. I have known for the past five years everything he has done—and I know all about you too, Shelley. I knew exactly what you looked like well before you arrived, your taste in clothes, in perfume — everything. Even about Alec Masters.'

She thought that she was going to faint. She tried to stand up, to escape, because this was a nightmare ... The room spun round, fast, faster, faster—and the next moment he was holding her in his arms.

CHAPTER FOUR

SHELLEY stood there helpless, supported by a pair of arms whose strength reached out and enfolded her and held her as she trembled and shivered with the shock of it all.

'Let me go,' she whispered. 'Please—let me go!'

'When you can stand alone,' he answered, and picked her up and carried her into her bedroom. He laid her down on the bed and pulled off her sandals, then went out. When he returned he was carrying a glass of water, and Shelley was sitting up.

'Why?' she asked. 'Why?'

'Because I knew, one day, I would have my chance to do to him what he did to me. My opportunity came the day you arrived. Only you weren't as I expected you to be. Not hard and brittle as I would have thought, but—vulnerable. When I put my proposition to you I already knew that the marriage would be in name only. I had to assure Victor of that, however.'

'Oh, God,' she said. 'The woman you once loved—the one you told me about. Was it my father who——'

'Yes,' he said harshly. 'And now you know the whole truth.'

'And you would have had the perfect revenge?'

'Yes.'

She closed her eyes. There were no more tears to shed. She had always known that her father had had many mistresses; he was an attractive man, who drew women, by a kind of cruel charm, like moths to a flame. He would have been amusing himself, taking a woman from a business rival, undoubtedly trying to find out secrets at the same time, using her as he used everybody else. She shivered, icily cold. She remembered the expression on Vargen's face when he had told her why he had no heart. And now, at last, she understood.

'Please go,' she said. Then she looked up at him. 'I'll be ready at seven.'

He stood up, and those cool hard eyes looked down at her. 'I had to tell you,' he said.

'And now you have. You only told me because there was the danger of my uncle telling me. Did you think I would go back on my word? I won't I promise you.' She looked down at her coverlet. 'Please go. I'd like to be alone.'

He walked out, and she heard the door close. She lay back on the bed and gazed up at the ceiling. Now, at last, she was clear in her mind. In a strange way, she was almost relieved that he had told her the truth. It wouldn't alter anything, because she had adjusted her mind to the acceptance of the mock marriage to escape from her father. There was also another reason why she had decided to go ahead, but she wasn't prepared to admit that to herself as yet. An image of Vargen's face came into her mind as she closed her eyes, and she remembered the strength of his arms around her. No one had ever held her like that. She knew that what was happening to her was impossible and unthinkable—but her heart was telling her otherwise.

She knew that if she ever allowed herself to fall in love with Vargen, she would be the loser when the six months had passed. She knew all this with the reasoning, logical part of her, and yet with another, deeper, more primitive part, she knew that she had never found a man so devastating as he. It was a magnetism, part love, part hate. She wanted to punish him for being as hard and ruthless as the father who had broken her heart so many years ago when she had discovered that he would never love her—and yet she wanted Vargen Gilev to take her and make love to her—to take her——

She sat up abruptly. Her mind had been clear only minutes before; now she felt as if she were going mad. She put her hand to her head, now throbbing with the pain of a sudden headache. Vargen Gilev didn't love her and never would. He didn't love anybody, perhaps not even himself. Slowly she walked over to her dressing table and sat down at the mirror. She took a long, hard look at herself, a cool assessing look. Her face looked back at her, a gently oval face, with a faint dimple in the chin, a tiptilted nose, wide-apart blue eyes, delicately shaped mouth. She touched her lips. She knew she had good features—the looks of too many men had told her so, their eyes warm upon her at social affairs with her father, and at parties—but she had never really believed the compliments bestowed on her. How could she be lovely when the most important person in her life didn't love her? But now the memories returned, and she wondered if perhaps she was beautiful after all. She smiled to herself, a hard, sad little smile. The bargain had been made. So be it. In six months, when she was free, she would learn how to live. Not until then. But until that time she would be the perfect wife, a robot to match the robot she was going to marry. A beautiful robot. She would earn the money he was going to pay her when she achieved her freedom, and he his.

She looked at her watch and made her plans for the rest of the afternoon. She wasn't going to go to the swimming pool, she was going to have her hair done at

the beauty salon in the hotel, then shower, and wear
the new evening dress she had bought that morning,
and which would surely be delivered soon; then she
would make herself up, and she would look devastatingly beautiful, and Vargen's godfather would be
bowled over and would assume that Vargen was madly
in love with her—and she would behave as if he were.
She ran her hands through her long silky hair and
smiled to herself. The headache was going. She wondered how Vargen would react when he saw her—
when he realised that she was going to be as hard as
him.

Shelley went over to the telephone. 'This is Miss
Regan in the Orange Suite,' she told the receptionist.
'I'd like to have my hair cut and styled as soon as possible, please. Ring me back, will you?' She was assured
of instant attention, and replaced the receiver. She had
seen a middle-aged American woman go into the beauty
salon the morning she arrived. She had also seen her
emerge two hours later looking quite stunning. The
new hair-style had done wonders. And it'll do wonders
for me, too, she thought. Tonight, the new Shelley will
emerge—and everyone will be surprised. Perhaps even
me.

It was ten minutes to seven and Shelley was ready. She
sat at the dressing table and applied the last coat of
lip-gloss. She looked absolutely perfect, she knew she
looked perfect, and she was waiting for Vargen to come
down for her. She had had her hair cut and shaped,
washed and blow-dried, and she looked completely
different, her face framed exquisitely and beautifully
by the gentle glossy style, much shorter than it had been,
and accentuating the delicate bone structure of her face.

the soft curve of her cheeks. She had spent several minutes applying her eye make-up the way a model friend had taught her, and the extra effort had been well worthwhile. Her eyes glowed lustrous and dark, her skin shone with health and the slight tan she had acquired over the last couple of days.

She sprayed her favourite perfume, a musky scent, over the pulse points and then stood up to go to the full-length mirror in the bathroom. The evening gown she had bought, a simple black sheath dress in wild silk, fitted her to perfection. It was backless, high-necked at the front with a diamanté choke collar. She wore no other jewellery. She looked at herself, and heard a knock at the outer door. Turning slowly, she walked into the lounge and stood there. 'Come in,' she called.

It was Vargen. She heard his footsteps, his voice, telling her, and then he entered the lounge. He looked at her, and for a moment it was as though time itself stood still; for one timeless moment there was nothing in the world save the two people facing each other across an hotel room.

Then he broke the silence, and the timeless moment shattered into a million shimmering fragments. 'You look very beautiful,' he said. 'Truly beautiful.'

Shelley gave a mock curtsey. 'Thank you.' A brittle smile accompanied the words. 'I decided to look different, so I went and had my hair cut.' She picked up her small silver evening bag from the table. 'I'm ready. Shall we go?'

'Your uncle is in my apartment,' he told her.

'And your godfather?'

'He will arrive later, with his wife. I thought we would have a drink with Victor first.'

'Of course.' She walked past him, then turned slightly in the doorway and looked at him. 'Oh, my perfume—I've forgotten——'

'Shall I get it?'

'Please. On the dressing table.' She waited. She was satisfied, so far. She had seen the shock in his eyes when he had first looked at her. It was enough for now. He might not be human, he might have no heart, but he had manners, and an undoubted magnetism, and as long as she kept a secret part of herself intact she would be safe. She might even enjoy this, the first evening of the masquerade. 'Thank you, Vargen.' She took the small phial of perfume from him and waited for him to open the outer door.

They took the lift up to his penthouse, where Uncle Victor was waiting by the window, glass in hand, admiring the view. He looked at her, stunned, then came forward and took her hands. 'My dear Shelley,' he said, 'you're quite ravishing! I wouldn't dare kiss you—you're too fragile-looking to touch.'

She laughed, leaned up, and kissed his cheek. 'No, I'm not. See? I must have a new style more often if that's what it does!'

'Shelley, what would you like to drink?' Vargen asked. A table had been converted into a small cocktail bar.

She surveyed the selection of drinks, then answered: 'Orange juice, please—and lots of ice.'

'Nothing stronger?' he raised an enquiring eyebrow.

She gave him a sweet smile. 'I intend to keep a clear head. Now, Uncle, let's talk, you and I.' She sat down on the settee by the window and Victor did the same. 'I'll be here for the next six months—you know our arrangement, of course,' she took the glass from Vargen,

'Thank you. Are you going to sit down?' She looked coolly, calmly at him.

'If you'll excuse me, I'll leave you to talk while I go and organise the dinner.'

'As you wish, of course.' She turned back to her uncle. 'Tell me your plans.'

They heard Vargen go quietly out, the door close, and Victor let out his breath in a long sigh. 'What's going *on*?' he whispered fiercely.

Shelley laughed. 'What *do* you mean?' Her eyes sparkled.

'You know damned well,' he growled. 'This new, cool, beautiful young woman sails in and it's you—but it's not the same girl I saw this afternoon at all.'

'Oh yes, it is, but I've had time to think, that's all.' She grinned at him. 'Two can play at this game, that's what I decided. Vargen's a cool customer—so will I be. Just watch me in action tonight and you'll see. We had quite a talk when we got back here this afternoon— and I saw a lot of things very clearly.' She patted his hand. 'And if I ever feel like screaming I'll run to you and pour it all out to you.'

'I hope you know what you're doing,' he said doubtfully.

'I do now. Don't you see? We'll both keep our side of the bargain and at the end of six months I'll be free. Free of him—and free of Father.' Her eyes were a little bright, and Victor, seeing it, squeezed her hand.

'My God, you're a bonny little fighter,' he said huskily. 'Charles is a fool, always has been. You're so like your mother, my dear—so like her. She was a beautiful, wonderful woman and I thank God you've grown up like her——' He stopped and looked away.

'Don't,' Shelley pleaded. 'Please, Uncle—I didn't

realise—don't spoil my new found cool. You'll have me crying in a minute!'

'Sorry!' He took a deep breath, then laughed. At least it was a good enough attempt at a laugh, and it sufficed. 'I think I'll have another drink. I don't think our host will mind, do you?'

'I'm sure not.' She looked round. 'I wonder how long he'll be?'

'I don't know. I came early and we had a talk before he went down for you. He's told me——' he stopped, then shook his head. 'Never mind. I feel better about this marriage. And having seen you tonight, I feel better still. Oh, Shelley, what a long time we've wasted! All these years—and I thought of you often. I wrote many times, but I don't suppose the letters ever reached you.'

'No,' she shook her head. 'Dad always had the post taken to him first. Is it any wonder? I'm sorry, though, I wish I'd known——'

'Never mind, you're here now. We'll make the most of your time here. We'll see each other often. I—er—do have someone I'd like you to meet, actually——' he hesitated.

Her eyes lit up. 'A lady friend?'

'Yes. Her name's Eileen, she's American, a writer, and a widow——'

'Oh, Uncle!' She hugged him impulsively, and he laughed.

'Whoa! Don't spoil your immaculate appearance.'

'Blow that! Are you going to marry her?'

'I haven't asked her yet——'

'Scared?'

'No,' he smiled. 'I wanted to get the hotel out of the way first. There's a villa on the other side of Avala I've got my eye on. Eileen's a writer, as I said, and it'll be ideal for her—and you know me, I enjoy doing a bit of painting.'

'I do. That's a talent I seem to have acquired from you, actually. I've always found I could relax dabbling with paints and canvas. Needless to say, Father thought it a waste of time,' she added wryly.

'Shall we make a promise not to talk about him?'

'Agreed.' They shook hands solemnly, then Vargen walked in.

'All is arranged,' he said. 'Bruno and Sophia will be here in half an hour, and dinner shortly after. Victor, another drink?'

'I just helped myself, thanks.' Victor held up his glass.

'Ah, good. Shelley? More orange juice?'

'No, thanks.' Vargen filled a glass for himself with vodka and went to the window. 'I hope you will come to the wedding, Victor—if you wish to.'

'I'd love to.' Victor smiled at Shelley.

'Can he bring a friend?' she asked.

'Certainly. It's to be a small affair, you understand, and the reception will be here afterwards. The wedding is at one in the civil registry office.'

'We'll be there.' Victor seemed as if he wanted to change the subject. Shelley sensed that while he had accepted the bizarre arrangement, it was not something he cared to dwell on, and she skilfully changed the conversation by asking Vargen for more ice in her drink, then adding:

'I'm looking forward to meeting Eileen, Uncle. Could we perhaps have lunch together tomorrow?' Then, with a long cool glance at Vargen: 'That is if you've nothing else planned for me?'

'No, I shall be very busy tomorrow. Perhaps you would like to have lunch up here, the three of you—as my guests?'

It wasn't at all what Shelley wanted, but the new cool Shelley wasn't going to say so. She lifted her glass. 'How very kind. Shall we meet here at one, Uncle?'

'Thank you. I'll arrange it with her.'

Shelley stood up and picked up her evening bag. 'Excuse me.' She sailed off towards the bathroom. Safely inside she locked the door and sank down on to the small stool, letting her breath out in a long 'Phew!' She looked across at herself in the mirror. 'It'll get easier as it goes along,' she told herself firmly. That helped. She managed to smile at her reflection. Of course it would. Victor was perfect. She had done the sensible thing in contacting him, she knew that now. He was warm and kind, and he cared for her—and he had written to her many times, only her father had made sure she never knew. Not surprising, really, after their row. Her father was a man who held grudges for many years—perhaps for ever. He had never been known to forgive anybody. His anger would be all the greater if—when —he found out she had contacted Victor. But she knew that there was now a warm bond between them, and perhaps always had been, even during the years of silence, the wasted years. If only Victor had been her father ... She stood up, restless and disturbed at the thought, and searched in her bag for her lip-gloss. It was better not to think like that. Better ...

She took a deep breath. She was looking forward to meeting Eileen. She already had a mental picture of her, and it would be interesting to see if it matched up to the reality. Shelley applied more lip-gloss where it had smudged slightly, dabbed perfume on her neck and wrists, and when she walked out a few moments later she was as cool and composed as before.

The room was softly lit, the windows wide open to

the cool evening air, and both men were talking quite amiably. Shelley drifted over and sat down beside her uncle. A moth fluttered against the shade of one of the lamps, and she watched it, letting the talk flow round her, talk of business, minor matters about her uncle's hotel, nothing that she felt concerned her. It left her free to think, and to watch Vargen without him being aware of it. He was dressed formally in white evening jacket, crisp white shirt, bow tie, slim-fitting black trousers. He was broad-shouldered, the jacket fitting him perfectly, emphasising the powerful build of him, the thick neck, the proud head. He looked at her now, as if aware of her eyes upon him.

'Forgive us—talk of business must be boring for you, Shelley.'

'I'll get used to it,' she responded calmly. 'Please don't stop on my account. I was deep in thought.'

'So I could see, but this is a social occasion, not a business meeting. Perhaps I had better give you some details of Bruno and Sophia. They are both French, and Bruno, my godfather, was my mother's cousin. I am very fond of them.'

Fond of someone? Vargen? Good heavens, she thought, but wisely said nothing. Victor excused himself, and for a few minutes she and Vargen were alone. She looked up at him. 'I shall be the perfect bride-to-be,' she said. 'You needn't worry that I'll let you down.' She raised her glass. 'Which is why I'm drinking fruit juice.'

'I'm sure you won't,' he answered smoothly. 'But does not a drink make you feel more relaxed?'

'Sometimes. I might have one later. Why, do you need a drink to help *you* relax?'

He looked at her. 'No.'

'I thought not,' she said, and felt the tension fill the room even as she did so. 'After all, you wouldn't would you?'

'Don't spoil it,' he remarked very quietly, and the threat lay behind the words, unspoken, but there. She felt her throat constrict.

'There's nothing to spoil. Everything's perfect,' she answered.

'Yes——' he began, and her uncle returned, and whatever else he had been going to say was lost. Then, shortly afterwards, Bruno and Sophia Lavelle arrived, and Shelley took a deep breath as they entered, and prepared to be the model bride-to-be.

Before she went to sleep that night, well after midnight, she reflected on the evening. Apart from the very slight brush with Vargen, it had indeed gone smoothly. Bruno, a stocky, grey-haired Parisian with shrewd brown eyes, had taken to Shelley immediately, and made it clear to everyone. His wife, Sophia, a cool sophisticated blonde in her mid-fifties, with an inborn chic, was quite charming, and had flirted gently with both Victor and Vargen while her husband paid court to Shelley. And Vargen had been the kind of host you read of in the glossy magazines. The evening had been a great success all round.

Vargen had escorted Shelley to her suite when at last it was over, opened her door for her and handed her her key. 'Goodnight, Shelley,' he had said. 'You bowled Bruno over completely.'

'I intended to,' she replied. 'It's part of the bargain, remember?' And she had smiled. 'Goodnight.' She had closed her door and gone in and collapsed on the bed and closed her eyes, seeing Vargen's face when she had said what she had. Not anger exactly. Not quite that, but—she shivered, remembering, now in bed, in the last few minutes before sleep claimed her. His expression, and particularly his eyes, had puzzled her. They were the last thing she saw before she fell asleep.

The following day, the last day before her wedding, was a busy one. She rose early and went swimming in the pool, which was practically empty. She saw Walter Grey after breakfast and told him that she had acquired the Hotel Catalina, that the auction was therefore cancelled, and that he might as well go home. He was nervous and uneasy, that was obvious. They sat in the foyer, where she had spotted him going out and called him back to let him know. She had a great deal of sympathy for him. When she had told him, she smiled. 'There's a flight at eleven tomorrow, I believe,' she said. 'You might as well catch it. Your job here is over.'

'I'm supposed to stay until Sunday, and see you go——' he began, unhappily.

'There's no point,' she told him gently. 'I'm staying on here for a while——' she held up her hand as he started to speak. 'There's nothing you could do about that, and my father won't blame you for it. Just tell him——' she racked her brains, searching for inspiration, and found it. 'Tell him you followed me to my uncle's hotel today and saw us talking. You can tell him that when you like.' She stood up. 'I'm sorry if I've given you a shock, but I'm telling you now to give you time to plan how you'll word things. I probably won't see you again, so goodbye, and good luck.' She shook hands with him, and went off to her room to begin the preparations for meeting Eileen.

They arrived promptly at one, and Shelley was waiting in Vargen's apartment for them. She had dressed in a blue cotton sundress, washed her hair after her swim, and was feeling good. As soon as Eileen walked in, Shelley knew she was going to like her. She was a green-eyed redhead with a slim, stunning figure and a warm smile—totally unlike the mental picture that Shelley had conjured up, but so very right for her uncle. They had shaken hands, started talking, and hadn't stopped throughout lunch. Eileen loved Victor, that was obvious. It was equally clear that he thought the world of her.

'Honey,' said Eileen, when they were going, 'we must keep in touch. Victor told me you were lovely, and he's right. When you come back from your honeymoon, can we get together for a girl talk?' This with a wink at Victor, who shrugged, pulled a face, and muttered something to the effect that he couldn't imagine what there was left to say, after their marathon conversation.

They both laughed, and Shelley hugged the other woman. 'I'd love to,' she answered. 'I'll see you at the wedding tomorrow, of course.' And to her uncle, as he went out, she whispered: 'You'd better marry her, I could do with an aunty like that!'

'I'll tell her.' He went off towards the private elevator, arm round Eileen, still chuckling. Shelley closed the door and surveyed the table. Time to ring for the waiters to come and clear away, then the afternoon was her own. She hadn't seen Vargen since the previous night. He had left a note for her, telling her to order the lunch when she needed it, and wishing them all a pleasant meal. It was signed simply 'V.'

She rang down to reception, then went over to the window. She opened the long sliding window and stepped out on to the small balcony. Looking down she could see her uncle getting into a car with Eileen. The road was busy and filled with noon-time traffic, and the air shimmered in the intense heat. In the distance the sea was as calm and level as molten metal, and further away still she could see small islands outlined only faintly in the heat mist. It was a beautiful day, but then it always was here on Avala. The hum of the traffic was distant and soothing. Shelley leaned her hands on the low stone wall of the balcony and watched a white-uniformed policeman waving his arms and blowing his whistle frantically at a red Volkswagen that had stalled on the crossing.

'Did the lunch go well?' She jumped round guiltily at the sound of the voice which came from behind her. Vargen had walked in silently and stood watching her from the window.

She put a hand to her pounding heart. 'I didn't hear you come in. I thought you were busy.'

'I was. I was at the desk when you rang down. I met your uncle and his friend on their way out. She is charming.' He walked out to stand beside her on the balcony.

'Yes, I know.' She looked at her watch. 'Thank you for the lunch, we enjoyed it very much. I'd better go now. I was just waiting for the staff to come and clear the table before going.'

'And what are you doing this afternoon?'

She glanced at him. 'I thought I'd go round the market. Why?'

'We have not yet bought our wedding rings.'

'I know. I forgot yesterday—I'm sorry.'

'Would you like to come out with me now?' he asked.

'But you said you had a lot to do today.'

'It is done. Now I am free. There is a jeweller's near by. It will not take long.'

'Of course it won't. They're only temporary anyway.' She smiled at him. 'There's no need for anything expensive.'

'Do you get pleasure from talking like this?' he asked in level tones.

Yes, I do, she wanted to say. She wanted to hurt him, to *hurt* him, only she couldn't. No one could. She turned away from him lest he see it in her eyes, and he caught her by the shoulders and twisted her round. 'Do you?' he repeated.

He was very near. She could see the smooth tanned skin, the tautness of his expression, and she experienced the desire to lash out, to scratch that skin, to see him bleed—she caught her breath. He had said that—he had said, 'Would you like to see me bleed?' She felt a shiver of apprehension and her eyes were wide as she stared at him.

'It's true, isn't it?' she demanded. 'It's only temporary, this—marriage.'

'But it will be done properly, you understand?'

'Let me go, you're hurting me!'

'No, I'm not. I don't understand you, Shelley. Last evening you were utterly charming. And yet now——'

'There were other people here. That's what it's all about, isn't it?' she said. 'A pretence, a game to impress Bruno—but we know the truth, don't we? We're alone now. I'll say what I like to you, do you hear? I'll say what I *like*!' She struggled to free herself, to push him away, but only succeeded in making him hold her more firmly.

'You little fool!' he grated, and dragged her into the lounge. She lashed out then as he released her and caught him a stinging slap on his face, then spun away, frightened.

'*Chort!*' he exclaimed. 'You would have fallen over the wall then, don't you see?' He strode over and shook her. 'Why do you think I dragged you in—to rape you? You could have gone over the top——' Shelley looked round, wide-eyed, saw the low stone balustrade, and realised the truth of his words.

'Oh no,' she murmured. 'Oh——' Vargen stopped shaking her and held her tightly to him.

'Did you think I was attacking you?' he said harshly. 'Did you?'

'Yes!' she gasped. 'I—I'm——' She shuddered helplessly, lifted her face to him, feeling the absolute strength of him, the sheer leashed power, so tightly controlled, and she was afraid of her own reaction. She wanted him to kiss her, she wanted—she wanted—— Tremulous, mouth trembling, eyes filling with helpless tears, she stood in the shelter of his arms and looked up at him, and whispered: 'I'm sorry, Vargen——' then she closed her eyes, because the fantasy, the imagining, was so real that it was as though she could already feel his mouth on hers. She was weak and helpless, trapped like a moth—then the fantasy became reality, and she felt the sensation of his lips on hers. Warm, firm, sensual, his mouth came down on her mouth. His arms, the hands that only seconds ago had been shaking her in anger, were sliding round her now, hard and strong, until they held her in a grip of steel, while his mouth teased and delighted her senses and her whole body melted into fire with the sensuality of a kiss that was like no other she had ever known.

Searching, deep, his breath on her face, his mouth a butterfly touch over her cheeks now, then her eyes, kissing her so gently, searching, reaching for her mouth again, and blending together as though they had been meant to meet since the beginning of time but losing all sense of time because it was timeless, it had no beginning and no end, it just was. Shelley moved her fingers to touch and caress the back of his neck, to feel the strength of him, and all sensation was there in her

fingertips and coursing through her very being and she
knew the truth of everything; it was like a door to
another world opening, a world she had never known
because everything was in that kiss; in the very existence of it was all the essence of lovemaking—it was as
complete as that. Their bodies had melted together,
Vargen's hard lean length against her softer feminine
curves, and there was no light, no time, no sound, only
the completeness of what was happening to them both.

They were not two separate people, they were one
being, breathing as one, hearts beating together, and
all was blended. She was filled with warmth, and golden
light, and fire, and she was going to stay there for ever,
for ever . . .

Thunder filled her head, exploding—and she was no
longer part of him. The knocking at the door registered
gradually, the thunder of her heart dying down as he
moved away, turned, said something to the man at the
door—she knew not what, she was past hearing words.
Vargen was no longer part of her being. She couldn't
look, she could scarcely move, yet she found the power
at last to do so, to walk into the bedroom, to the bathroom. There her limbs failed her and she collapsed on
to the stool trembling in every fibre of her body. She
knew now what her mind had tried to deny before.

She knew that she loved Vargen Gilev.

CHAPTER FIVE

SHELLEY sat on the bed, listening to the voices and the clatter of crockery from the lounge. She wasn't going to go out yet, because she couldn't. Then a door opened, and was shut, and there was silence. She wondered if Vargen had followed the waiters out. It didn't seem to matter. He might just leave her there. What had happened was more explosive than if he had made love to her. It had been a lovemaking in a kiss. It had been so complete that nothing could follow and not be an anticlimax. She understood now all the love poems she had read and never fully comprehended. Now, they had sense and a full meaning. Now, she knew. At last she knew all that had been hidden all her life.

She lay back on the bed and kicked off her sandals and closed her eyes. Warmth and colour and light filled her head, dancing colours in fantasy patterns. When his voice came from by the door, she opened her eyes to see him standing there and smiled sleepily, dreamily, seeing the man she loved. The light was in her eyes, the light of the love that shone out.

'Forgive me,' he said.

She sat up. 'There's nothing to forgive. Come over here,' she smiled. She was very happy.

He remained where he was. 'We had better go now.'

'Go? Where?' She was confused. Didn't he *know*? Couldn't he *see*?

'For the rings.'

'Then help me up,' she whispered—and saw his face change.

'No,' he answered. He was holding on to the door, and she began to laugh, because she still didn't realise.

'Are you frightened of me?' she asked.

'No.'

'Then come over here and help me up.'

He turned and went out. An icy cold sensation washed over her as she saw him go, and the love, the warm happy feelings, vanished like mist in the sun.

Shelley stood up very slowly and went to the door, forgetting her sandals. Vargen was standing outside it, his back to her. She touched his arm. 'Look at me,' she whispered. He turned slowly and looked down at her, towering over her as she stood there barefoot. Then she saw the contempt in his eyes and caught her breath in sudden unbearable pain. 'Oh, God!' she murmured, and moved back as though he had struck her. It was as though he actually had. His expression, the contempt she saw, were like a blow to her heart. She turned away and stumbled over to the bed for her sandals. Her hands shook as she tried to put them on, and she had to sit down on the bed or she would have fallen. She felt unclean, soiled by his touch, so great was the sense of rejection. The tears ran unheeded down her face as she fastened the straps on her sandals. She wanted so badly to hurt him as he had just hurt her that she put her hand to her mouth to stop herself crying out with the pain of it.

He came in carrying a glass. 'Water,' he said.

Shelley took it from him and flung the contents in his face. Then she stood up. Taking a deep breath, fighting for control, she said: 'Yes, we'd better go.'

He wiped the water from his face, and she laughed. 'You'd better dry off first, though,' and she flung the empty glass across the room, where it shattered against the wall in the corner. She saw a muscle move in his cheek, and stared at him, eyes bright, heedless of the tears that were now drying. 'Let's get this farce over,' she said. 'Let's go and choose the rings.' She walked past him and into the lounge. Very steadily down the steps she went, biting her lip hard to keep from crying again. If he didn't see, it wouldn't matter. It must not matter, or she was lost.

She took out her comb and flicked her hair back, and waited for him. She didn't look at him again. When she heard him following she went to the outer door, and was about to open it when his arm came out and held it shut.

'Wait,' he said, 'Shelley——' he touched her arm.

That did it. She whirled round, breast heaving. 'Don't *touch* me,' she breathed. 'Don't touch me ever again!' She stared at him with hate in her eyes. 'You make my flesh creep when you touch me—do you understand?' Her cheeks were flushed, her eyes wide and bright. 'The—the arrangement doesn't cover touching, does it?' When he didn't answer she struck him so hard that it hurt her hand. His head jerked sideways and she felt a surge of satisfaction that was so strong it nearly made up for the rejection and the contempt she had seen in his face.

She had hurt him, she could see that, see the mark blazing on his cheek before fading. She flung the door open and went out, and walked very steadily, very carefully towards his private elevator. It was going to be all right. She would be safe if she controlled herself, safe from further humiliation. She had let him see, hadn't she? Let him see that she didn't care about the kiss. He *had* to see.

She pressed the button and the elevator door opened instantly. She stepped in, and as the elevator went down she opened her bag and applied fresh lipstick with a nicely steady hand. Vargen might not have been there. She neither looked at him or spoke.

Outside, on the blazing hot street, he pointed. 'This way.' He was careful not to touch her. It would have been natural, in any other circumstances, for him to take her arm when he pointed, or even when they crossed the traffic-filled street, but he made sure that he didn't. Shelley couldn't see if he was angry or contemptuous, because she didn't once look at him. She looked at the crowds of people, at the passing cars and pony traps, at the beautiful buildings, but she didn't want to look at Vargen.

She walked into the cool jeweller's shop and they were ushered into a private room where several trays of rings were produced for their inspection. Then they were alone. Presumably he knew the owner—he might even *be* the owner. She neither knew nor cared, she only wanted to get it over with as soon as possible. A wedding ring was supposed to be very important, but a brass curtain ring would have done. She tried a few on, found one that fitted, said to Vargen: 'This will do,' and put it down on the glass-topped counter. The ring was a wide plain one. She looked with complete uninterest as he tried on several to match hers, but much larger.

'Can I go now?' she asked, when he found one.

'Where are you going?'

'Does it matter?' She looked at him, her face expressionless.

'No.'

'I'm free to go where I want?'

'Of course. But I would have sent a car for you had you wished.'

'I don't need one, thank you. I prefer to walk.'

She waited as he spoke to the assistant, then they

were outside again, the two rings in boxes in her handbag. 'Goodbye,' she said, and walked away, leaving him standing outside the shop. She didn't look back. Soon she was in the market, and there the noise and the bustle helped her to get back to normality. It was too crowded and colourful for her to be otherwise. She was jostled in the throng of eager tourists and visitors buying their souvenirs to take home to families and friends, and Shelley herself found a stall selling cushions and tablecloths where she bought a colourfully embroidered cloth for her old nanny. The old lady loved pretty things, and lived in a flat crammed with ornaments and vases and old musical boxes that Shelley loved to play when she visited.

She bought an ice cream from a stall, and wandered along licking it, pausing to study a stall crammed with lengths of beautiful silks and lace. Time passed, and she began to feel much calmer. Six months wasn't forever. It would soon pass. And in a few years her visit to Avala would be no more than a memory.

'Sorry——' she said instinctively as she was bumped by a man, and his apology came immediately after hers. He was tall and blond—and American, as she discovered when he spoke again a moment later.

'Hey, don't apologise. It was all my fault.'

She nodded, smiling at him, and walked away—and he followed. 'Hey, ma'am, can I buy you a drink to make up for my bad manners in nearly knocking you over?'

'No, thanks. And you didn't, really.'

'Look, all right, so I didn't nearly knock you over— but please have a drink anyway. There's a bar over yonder.'

Why not? she thought. 'All right, thank you. Just one.'

He took her parcel and pushed a way for her through the crowds, and into a small dimly lit bar. There he sat her at a table by the window and said: 'Don't vanish, I'll be back.'

A moment later he returnèd, bearing two tall glasses. 'Two Avala Specials,' he grinned. 'My name's Dave Mannering, I'm from Illinois, I'm thirty, and I'm not married.'

'Phew! A life story in one sentence. Well done.' She raised her glass. 'Cheers!'

'Cheers. You are English, of course? On vacation here?'

'Sort of. My name's Shelley.'

'Shelley—lovely name. What goes with it?'

'Just Shelley will do.' She smiled at him. 'Are you staying on the island, Dave?'

'Only for today. I'm on the liner *Carina*, on a cruise. If I'd known I was going to meet you I'd have changed my plans.'

She laughed. 'I'll bet you're having a good time aboard ship.'

'Well——' he grinned, 'not bad at all. Tell me about yourself though, Shelley. What made you come here? Where are you staying? And are you married?'

'I'll take the last question first. I will be tomorrow.'

'Married? Oh, jeez, I knew it! Just my luck. Er——' he looked round him in mock nervousness, 'he's not hovering around, is he?'

'I doubt it,' she answered. It was almost funny.

'What's he thinking of, letting you wander off then? I sure as hell wouldn't.'

'You're not my fiancé, though.'

He had kind, friendly eyes, and he looked at her now, and there was warmth in them. 'I should have known! You've got that look about you, honey, all glowing, you know? He's a lucky man—you must love him a lot. I'd like to meet him.'

'You can do. He's just walked in,' she answered, surprised at how calmly she managed to say it. Vargen stood just inside the doorway, unsmiling, and Dave Mannering rose to his feet. As Vargen walked towards them Shelley said quickly: 'Vargen, meet Dave. Dave—Vargen, my fiancé.'

Dave extended his hand, as did Vargen. And if Dave was disconcerted he managed not to show it. 'Howdy. I was just sayin' I'd bet you weren't far away. I hope you don't mind me asking Shelley for a friendly drink —I nearly knocked her over in the crush outside. It was the least I could do.'

'Not at all.' Vargen smiled in a pleasant, controlled manner at the younger man. 'But if you'll excuse us now, Dave? We have an urgent appointment.'

'Sure. Nice to have met you both. And best wishes for tomorrow.'

'Thank you.' Shelley was inwardly seething, but not for anything would she let the friendly American see. Vargen had followed her, actually *followed* her! She shook his hand. 'And thanks for the drink. Goodbye, enjoy your cruise.'

'I'll try.' He watched them walk out, then sat down again with a wry grin.

Outside, Shelley turned on Vargen. 'Frightened to let me out of your sight?' she demanded icily. 'I wasn't going to run off with him, you know.' She stalked away, out of the market and towards the hotel, but he caught up with her.

'Calm down,' he said, his voice low and cold. 'I went to find you, yes, but I didn't follow you as you seem to think. You had mentioned before that you were going to the market. I came to find you only because there has been a telephone call for you.'

She stopped. 'What?'

'A call from your father—you never phoned him last night.'

'Oh! I forgot.' She went inwardly panicky for a second before she realised that it didn't matter. It would never matter again. 'And is that why he phoned —and why you came to tell me?'

'No. Grey must have called him this lunchtime to say you'd been to see your uncle, and bought the hotel.'

'Damn!' She hadn't thought he would telephone so quickly. The call would have reached her father at breakfast. He would wonder what on earth was going on, and well he might. The auction would only have taken place, had it been going to, minutes before. 'I'd better go and phone him now.'

'He said he'd wait,' Vargen told her.

'Did you speak to him?'

'Yes. The receptionist put it through immediately to me, knowing that you were out.'

'Did he know he was speaking to you?'

'No. I told him I was the owner. He was too angry to bother who he was speaking to.'

'He would be.' She began walking again, but more slowly. This would be the first real test of her courage. She wished suddenly that she had never come to Avala —then took the thought back. Because for one thing alone, it had been worth it. She had met Uncle Victor again. That, and that alone, made it worthwhile.

'What will you tell him?' he asked.

She shrugged. 'I'll think of something.' They were nearing the hotel and a party of Americans were coming out, laughing, enjoying themselves, and they had to wait a moment before going into the cool foyer. 'I'll go up to my suite,' she told him, and walked across to the elevator. When she reached it she looked back. Vargen was crossing to the reception desk. She had assumed that he would go up with her, and was perversely annoyed that he hadn't.

She was whisked up in the high-speed elevator by the operator, Manuel, who had treated her like royalty ever since news of her impending wedding to Vargen had leaked out. She smiled and thanked him as he ushered her out at her floor, and he beamed. 'Thank *you*, madame. Have a nice day.'

'And you, Manuel.'

In her lounge, Shelley flung her bags down on the chair and picked up the phone. Her mouth had gone dry. She asked for an outside line, dialled, and the telephone at the other end was picked up at the second ring. She could picture him sitting in his study, at his large paper-laden desk, hand outstretched for her call.

'Shelley?' He wasted no time on preliminaries. 'What the hell's going on there?'

'I've bought the Hotel——' she began.

'The auction's supposed to be *now*. What do you mean, you bought it—and how much? And what's this about you seeing Victor?' His voice shook with rage.

'How did you know that?' she asked. Her strength was growing. She hadn't thought it would, but she was realising suddenly that her father's terrifying anger no longer had the power to frighten her.

'Never mind how I know—I do, that's all—and I don't like your tone!'

'You know, Father, I had a pleasant surprise just now. I recognised a man from your office staying at this hotel. What a coincidence! He must be here on holiday. I'll see him later and give him the deeds to bring to you——'

'Bring?' Charles Weldon's voice rose. 'Bring? You're coming back with them!'

'No. I'm staying here for a while, Father.'

Shelley thought the telephone would explode, and held it away from her ear, wincing at the blast of anger vibrating down the line.

'You're getting home, girl—tomorrow!'

She took a deep breath as his voice raged on, telling her what she was to do, and precisely when, mapping out her actions for her, assuring her that if she disobeyed she would regret it, telling her that seeing Victor was the most foolish thing she could have done and he wanted to know what madness had overcome her. She held the telephone receiver at a distance of several inches from her, letting the words wash over her, realising that her father was almost beside himself with anger and guessing shrewdly that the main reason was that she was several thousand miles away and outside his direct control.

'You *hear* me?' he finished. 'Are you *there*?'

'Yes, I'm here,' she answered quietly.

'I'm phoning your hotel when I've finished with you. I shall tell them you're leaving tomorrow, that the bill will be paid up till then and no longer——'

'That doesn't matter, I've moved my room anyway. I'm in a suite now. You're not in charge any longer, Father, do you understand? I'm here, I'm staying here, I'm not coming home, and nothing you say can alter that.'

'You've gone mad!' His voice quivered with shock.

'Probably. Or maybe I've seen things clearly for the first time in my life. I've had a long talk with Uncle

Victor. I didn't realise he'd written to me so many times. You shouldn't have stolen his letters——'

The telephone went dead. Shelley heard him bang the receiver down, and she hung up. She was exhausted, as though she had been through an ordeal of fire. She put her head in her hands and took a few deep breaths. What if he took a plane and arrived here? The thought was dreadful—but it was a possibility. She would not put anything past him. He was never to be thwarted in any way, and she had just delivered a shocking blow to him.

She picked up the telephone again, and forcing herself to speak slowly and calmly asked the receptionist for Mr Gilev. She was put through immediately, which confirmed her thought that he had been waiting at the reception desk.

'Hello, Shelley.'

'Can you come up?' she asked.

'I'm on my way.' The telephone went dead. She went to open the outer door, returned to the lounge, poured herself a drink of Bacardi and Coke, and waited. Vargen arrived a minute later.

'He was very angry,' she said. 'What if he gets on a plane and comes here?'

'Is it possible that he will?'

'With him—yes, I'm afraid it is.'

Vargen looked at her. For a moment it seemed that there was a bond between them, a bond of mutual conspiracy. Shelley could almost feel the strength of him. She wanted to lean on him, to have him hold her securely against the world. But she had told him never to touch her again, and she knew that he would not. Whatever had happened that morning would not be repeated. In one sense they were united, in another there was a wide unbreachable gulf between them.

'Do you want to get married today?' he asked quietly.

She stared at him, wide-eyed. 'Today?' she whispered. 'But how——'

'It can be arranged. It needs several phone calls, that is all. It is—let me see'— he glanced at his watch— 'nearly three now.' He looked at her, eyes cool and hard. 'We can have the wedding at six. Then there is nothing anyone can do.'

She sat down. 'Three hours,' she whispered. Mentally geared to a wedding the following day, it was a shock to hear his calm words. Three hours away, that was all it need be. She looked up at him.

'The choice is yours, Shelley,' he said very quietly.

She nodded. 'Very well. Yes——' the words were very faint.

'Leave it to me. Will you stay here, where I can contact you?'

'Yes.' She ran her tongue over her dry lips. 'I—I'll start getting ready now.'

'Very well.' He walked out, and she was alone. In three hours she would be Mrs Vargen Gilev. It didn't seem possible. She stood up and went over to the wardrobe where her wedding dress hung and looked at it. Then, remembering, she opened her handbag and took out the two ring boxes. She would have to give her ring to Vargen. She opened the box containing his wedding ring and took it out. It was wider, larger and heavier than her own. She held it in her hand and looked at it, and a tear fell on it. Very carefully she put it down on the table, and went to run a cool shower.

When Vargen worked, he worked quickly. Within half an hour Pelma and Rose arrived at Shelley's suite carrying a huge bunch of flowers and a smaller bouquet of white freesias, which they put in Shelley's refrigerator. Pelma arranged the larger colourful bunch in a vase, and Rose gave Shelley a brilliant smile. 'We've come to help you,' she told her.

'How did you know it was today?' asked Shelley, bewildered. She had completely forgotten their offer of assistance.

'Mr Gilev phoned the store and told us of the change of plan, and could we come now,' Rose answered. 'And we are so pleased to do. Pelma will attend to any calls while I do your hair. It looks lovely, madame. Did you have it done at the salon in this hotel?'

'Yes.' Bemused, Shelley nodded.

'My cousin,' Rose beamed. 'He is good, yes?'

'He certainly is.' Shelley allowed Rose to lead her to the bedroom as the telephone shrilled behind them, and Pelma answered it. She followed them in.

'It is Mr Gilev,' she said. 'He told me to tell you that everything is organised. He has spoken to your uncle, and to Monsieur Lavelle as well, and they will be there. He says also that he would like your ring. He is sending someone up for it.'

'It's on the table.'

Shelley was glad they had arrived. She no longer felt alone. Both girls were efficient and helpful, taking all the worry from her, answering the door and the telephone while Shelley sat in a daze, letting it all happen. And when they discovered that she hadn't eaten since breakfast, Pelma sent down for sandwiches and coffee, which turned out to be just what she needed. She had begun to feel faint, and the wafer-thin chicken sandwiches made her feel better almost immediately, as did the strong coffee.

At five there was yet another knock at the door, a

hurried brief whispering in the hallway, and Rose returned bearing a small wrapped box which she handed
to Shelley.

'From Mr Gilev,' she said, and hovered by as Shelley
opened the box to reveal a bracelet and necklace of
diamonds set in gold. They glittered and sparkled fire
as she held the box up, and Rose gasped: 'Pelma, come
and see!'

Both girls stood there gaping while Shelley lifted out
the slender gold chain with the brilliant diamonds set
in it at intervals. It was absolutely beautiful, shimmering with a life of its own, as seemingly fragile as a
spider's web, delicate and exquisite.

'Oh, madame!' Rose whispered. 'Oh, I've never seen
anything quite so lovely.' Shelley herself was shaken.
The gift—if it was a gift—had taken her completely by
surprise. There was no note with the box.

'They are gorgeous,' she agreed.

'Let me help you put the necklace on,' said Pelma.
Shelley handed it to her and went over to the mirror
and Pelma fastened it on her. She looked at her reflection, and touched the fragile chain with gentle
fingers. The points of the diamonds caught the light as
her pulse beat in her throat, and shimmered and
dazzled. Then she put the bracelet on.

'Oh, you'll look *lovely*!' breathed Rose, clasping her
hands. 'Now it's time to put your dress on, and then
we'll help you to make up if you like.'

'Yes, it is time.' Shelley let them help her on with the
dress, let them cover her shoulders with a large towel,
let them sit her down at the dressing table, and she still
felt dazed. It was like a dream, as though it were happening to someone else, as though she were an onlooker
to a scene that really had nothing to do with her.

When, at five-thirty, the telephone rang again, and

Rose answered it and said, 'It's for you, madame, it's your father,' Shelley rose and went over to the phone, took it from her, and said:

'Will you leave me for a moment, please?' She waited until they had gone into the bedroom, then spoke. 'Hello, Father.'

'Are you coming home tomorrow, or do I have to come and fetch you?'

She took a deep breath. The sense of total unreality still filled her. 'You'd be too late if you did,' she said. 'I'm getting married in half an hour, and I won't be here when you arrive anyway.' There was no sound, nothing. She thought they must have been cut off. It didn't seem important. Very gently she replaced the receiver, and called out: 'You can come back in now. I'm ready.'

She wondered how many telephone calls her father had made before ringing her back, and if he had spoken to Vargen and what he had said if he had. She would know soon enough.

'We'll check what time the car will be coming for you, madame,' said Rose, and picked up the telephone.

'Thank you for all you've done,' said Shelley. 'I honestly don't know how I'd have coped without you.'

'It's our pleasure,' Pelma beamed at her. 'Mr Gilev asked if we'd like to help at the reception afterwards.'

'Did he? I'm glad.'

'Yes, we both had to phone home and tell our parents we'd be late. We wouldn't miss it for worlds.'

'Then I shall see you there.'

'We'll tidy up here first, with your permission, and then go up to Mr Gilev's apartment.'

'Of course.' Shelley looked across the room at Rose, who was on the telephone listening, nodding occasionally. Then she put the receiver down.

'The car will be here at ten to six. Mr Gilev has just left in it. They'll telephone up when it arrives back.'

Shelley didn't want to sit down and crease her dress, so she went over to the window and looked down to the colourful, crowded street below. It was all so unreal; everything was. The sounds from below came only faintly, as though in a film, then she saw the familiar shape of the long limousine snaking through the traffic, slowing as it neared the front of the hotel, and turned away. 'I think the car's here. I'd better take my flowers now.' She picked up the ring box containing Vargen's ring, took the small bouquet from Rose, and thanked her.

'We'll be thinking of you,' Rose said shyly, 'and we'll be waiting in Mr Gilev's apartment.'

Shelley wondered if they knew of Vargen's reputation with women—if indeed they actually knew any of his mistresses and ex-mistresses. It seemed very probable that they would. They were waiting, Rose near the telephone ready for the message about the car, Pelma kneeling to remove some minute pieces of thread from the hem of Shelley's wedding dress.

Then the telephone shrilled. Rose answered, said: 'Yes, right,' and put the receiver down. 'The car is waiting for you outside,' then: 'Ooh, madame, it's so *exciting*!' She put her hand to her mouth. 'Sorry,' she whispered.

Shelley laughed. 'Don't apologise. I'm just very glad you'll be at the reception. Thank you again for being here. I'll see you soon.'

They watched her leave, the elevator waited, door open, Manuel beaming, and Shelley walked slowly towards it. She was going to her wedding.

There was a dreamlike sensation that persisted

throughout the simple ceremony and stayed with her as they drove back to the hotel, she in the first car with Vargen, their four guests following in Bruno's Rolls, and it was still with the same feeling of unreality that she walked into Vargen's apartment—*their* apartment now—and waited for the others to arrive.

Rose and Pelma shyly greeted them, were thanked by Vargen for their help, then asked if they would ring down for the drinks and meal to be brought up.

Bruno and Sophia came in, followed by Victor and Eileen, there were kisses all round, and the apartment assumed a festive air as waiters arrived with laden dinner wagons, glasses were filled, and the two older women drifted over to the window with Shelley while the men stayed talking by the makeshift bar. Eileen raised her glass of champagne and smiled happily at Shelley and Sophia.

'Here's to the lovely bride,' she said. Whether she knew the truth, whether Victor had told her, was impossible to say. If she did know, nothing of it showed; she seemed genuinely delighted to be there. Sophia too raised her glass and smiled at Shelley.

'Yes, to you, and to Vargen,' she said. 'May you both have many years of happiness, my dear.'

'Thank you.' It would soon be over. Already it was growing dark outside, lights beginning to gleam from all over the island. The arrangements were made. Shelley and Vargen would spend the night in the apartment and the following morning they would leave on his yacht for a brief honeymoon. A sham honeymoon —but only three, possibly four people knew that. Shelley sipped her champagne and wondered how much of it she would have to drink before nothing would matter. She smiled, she responded, and she knew that she looked cool and beautiful because the mirror told her so, but inside she was totally numbed and unfeeling, because it wasn't really happening to her, she was only acting out a part.

An hour, two hours passed. They ate, they drank, everyone was happy and laughing. Vargen was courteous and charming, and Shelley drank the champagne as though it were water and remained cool and self-possessed, the radiant bride.

At last, it was over. Victor and Eileen left first. Shelley kissed and hugged them both and saw the traces of tears in her uncle's eyes, and whispered, at the door, so that no one else heard: 'It's going to be all right.'

Then Bruno and Sophia took their leave, smiling, relaxed, the waiters cleared away, and Rose and Pelma were sent off home by car, smiling and happy and both clutching envelopes that Vargen had given to them. Shelley looked round as the last waiter went out, and watched the door close quietly after him. Vargen poured her a glass of champagne and she took it from him and drank it in one go.

Now she knew that it was not a dream. She was here, it was all real. She was a married woman. And she was alone for the first time with her husband.

CHAPTER SIX

'I'D like some more champagne,' Shelley said. Vargen looked at her and smiled slightly.

'Don't you think you've had enough?' he said mildly.

'No. Why? Have you been counting the glasses?'

He shook his head. 'I can tell by your eyes.'

'Can you? How clever! Are you going to give me one or shall I pour it for myself?'

He picked up the bottle and she held her glass out. 'Thank you,' she said, and gave him a radiant smile. 'I'm going to bed soon. Where are you sleeping?'

'On the small bed in my dressing room. We leave at nine in the morning.'

'I'll be ready.' She emptied her glass. 'I'm going to read in bed for a while.'

'As you wish, of course,' he nodded. 'Is there anything you need?'

She looked steadily at him for a moment. 'From you?' A little smile. 'No. Goodnight.'

'Goodnight, Shelley.' He stood and watched her go.

She realised that all her clothes were downstairs in her suite when she was naked in the shower. There was a blue silk dressing gown hanging on the door in the bathroom, and she dried herself and put it on. It was far too long, and she had to roll up the sleeves, but it would suffice until she could send someone down in the morning for her own things. She belted it securely at the waist and walked barefooted into the bedroom, went over to the bookcase near the bed, and skimmed her eyes over the titles. Most of the books looked extremely boring, about finance and property, two were in Russian, several in French, but there were also some paperback novels which she lifted out and put on the bed.

She slid into bed, pulled the second pillow across and sat propped up. It was her wedding night, and she was spending it alone with a book. She began to laugh at the absurdity of it all, then the laughter changed, and she sobered, and picked up the first book and opened it. The print blurred and danced so that she could hardly read the title. She flung it aside and lay back and closed her eyes. She could hear no sounds from anywhere. She was thirsty, and she was wide awake. She got out of bed, retied the belt firmly and went across to the door and opened it. The lounge was empty, and only one lamp remained lit. Shelley went quietly down the three steps and crossed to the window.

The half empty champagne bottle stood on the table with the two glasses. She poured some out, it was warm and slightly flat, but she drank it anyway and then looked around. Had Vargen gone to bed—or gone out? If he was in he would surely have gone to the bathroom before going to bed, but she had heard no sounds. She felt as if she were alone in the apartment, and she had to find out. Quietly she walked into the bathroom and opened the second door, the one which led into the smaller room she had only once seen. It was empty. She closed the door and went back into the lounge, sat on the settee, poured herself the last of the champagne, and gazed out of the window.

How stupid she was not to have guessed! He had gone out, and he would stay out for as long as he chose, because this was a marriage in name only, and he was a man who needed women—he had told her that. In a strange way it was the reason he had married her. She wondered what he would look like when he returned. Satisfied? Content? She gripped the glass tightly, clenching her teeth to fight the wave of sick jealousy that washed over her. Oh, God, she hated him! He would be with some woman now, kissing her, murmuring words of love—words that he would never mean.

She turned her head in anguish from side to side. She was alone, she had always been alone, but this, now, was more agonising and poignant than ever before. The expression on Vargen's face after he had kissed her that morning returned to haunt her with the vivid images of her own agony. He had despised himself for his own weakness—and he had despised her: that had been made only too clear.

She leaned back on the settee and wondered how she would get through the night. He would surely return before breakfast. He had said that they were leaving at nine. He wouldn't let everyone know the true state of affairs by staying out all night. Perhaps he would only be an hour or so. Shelley found that her head was beginning to ache, a persistent throbbing pain across her temples that sent dazzling lights flashing in front of her eyes every time she blinked. She put her feet up, sat back more comfortably, and closed her eyes, knowing now that she wasn't going to go to bed until Vargen returned, and knowing too that she wouldn't sleep until he did, and perhaps not even then. The first night was the worst. After this she would learn to get used to it. She might even learn not to mind. It was only for six months, after all ...

She awoke from a confused dream, and it was light outside, and someone had covered her with a sheet, and put a pillow under her head, and the sun was shining in on her face now. Shelley sat up, dazed, and looked around her. She must have slept, after all—but where was Vargen? She stumbled to her feet and went into the bedroom. It was empty, the books still lying on the bed where she had left them. She went through the bathroom and into the small room, and Vargen lay asleep on a narrow bed.

She saw the clock on the wall; it was after six. He lay almost uncovered, and from the waist up he was naked. His body was hard, muscular, and tanned. Shelley stood and watched him, unable to look away, fascinated by the strength of him even when asleep. Black hair covered his chest and forearms, and his cheeks and chin were dark with beard shadow. He slept deeply, lying on his back, one arm outflung across the pillow, the wedding ring gleaming on his finger. Shelley shuddered with revulsion and turned away—and suddenly he was awake.

'Shelley?' He sat up.

She paused in the doorway. 'Yes?'

'You were asleep on the settee when I came in. I didn't like to wake you, so I put a sheet over you——'

'I know. Thank you. Did you have a nice time?'

'I was working.'

She stared at him. 'Is that what you call it?' She turned and went out, through the bathroom, the bedroom, and into the small kitchen where she put the kettle on and began to look in the cupboards for coffee. Vargen followed her in, fastening the belt on his trousers, still barefoot.

'Have you any aspirins or anything?' she asked. 'I've got a headache.'

'Yes.' He reached past her and handed her a bottle. 'Are you making coffee?'

'Yes. Do you want one?' She must remember the new, cool Shelley. She must keep her part of the bargain. It

A Home Subscription! It's the easiest and most convenient way to get every one of the exciting Harlequin Romance Novels!

...and you'll get 4 of them FREE

You pay nothing extra for this convenience, there are no additional charges...you don't even pay for postage!

Fill out and send us the handy coupon now, and we'll send you 4 exciting Harlequin Romance novels absolutely FREE!

Send no money, get these

four books FREE

Mail this postpaid coupon today to:

Harlequin Reader Service

901 Fuhrmann Blvd., Buffalo, N.Y. 14203

YES, please start a *Harlequin Romance* home subscription in my name, and send me FREE and without obligation my 4 *Harlequin Romances*. If you do not hear from me after I have examined my 4 FREE books, please send me the 6 new *Harlequin Romances* each month as soon as they come off the presses. I understand that I will be billed only $7.50 for all 6 books. There are no shipping and handling nor any other hidden charges. There is no minimum number of books that I have to purchase. In fact, I can cancel this arrangement at any time. The first 4 books are mine to keep as a FREE gift, even if I do not buy any additional books.

CR982

NAME

ADDRESS

CITY   STATE   ZIP CODE

This offer expires March 31, 1981. Prices subject to change without notice.
Offer not valid to present subscribers.

Printed in Canada.

Get your
Harlequin Romance
Home Subscription NOW!

- Never miss a title!
- Get them first—straight from the presses!
- No additional costs for home delivery!
- These first 4 novels are yours FREE!

FIRST CLASS
PERMIT NO. 8907
Buffalo, N.Y.

BUSINESS REPLY MAIL
No postage necessary if mailed in the United States.

Postage will be paid by

Harlequin Reader Service
901 Fuhrmann Blvd.
Buffalo, N.Y. 14203

would be such an effort at first, but she must succeed, or make herself ill.

'Please.'

'I had to borrow your dressing gown because I'd forgotten my own clothes.'

'I see. I'll have them sent up here before we leave.'

He sat down on a yellow-topped stool and watched her, and Shelley was suddenly aware that the dressing gown provided less than adequate covering. The material was so smooth and slippery that it kept sliding open. She turned away ostensibly to check the kettle, and took the opportunity to fasten the tie belt more securely around her slender waist. She looked down. The gown gaped open at the top, revealing the soft swell of her breasts, but there was nothing she could do about that because there were no buttons to fasten and it didn't matter anyway because whatever kind of woman attracted him, it wasn't her. It would never be her. She would be safe even if she took the dressing gown off and stood naked in front of him. He had more or less told her that when they had made the arrangements for the wedding, and he had certainly confirmed it by his actions yesterday.

She made the coffee and handed him his cup. Then she took two of the aspirins. She slid on to the other stool, careless of the fact that the long length of her legs was revealed, and sipped the hot coffee slowly, enjoying it as it brought her back to being fully awake. Her legs were getting nicely tanned, she noticed, and she slid her hand down one, casually carelessly. 'Will I be able to sunbathe on the boat?' she asked.

'Yes, of course, if you wish to. Do you have suntan lotion?'

She shrugged, and the top of the robe slipped slightly

towards her shoulder. She hooked it up again unselfcon-
sciously. 'I don't think I remembered to bring any.'

'Then I shall get some before we leave.' She looked
across at him. His eyes were very steady upon her. She
wondered if he even saw her as a woman. He wasn't
looking at her in the same way the friendly American
had done—but then if he'd just come from another
woman's arms, no doubt he had other things to think
about. Shelley rose gracefully from her stool and the
gown billowed open at top and hip. She turned away,
not quickly but not slowly either.

'I'll go down and get some clothes from my suite,' she
said, and went towards the door.

'Like that?'

She turned, slowly, standing in the doorway, and
smiled. 'Sorry? Like what?'

'Dressed in my gown?'

She looked down, pulled it more tightly round her,
then ran her fingers through her hair. 'Is that better?'

'I would rather you didn't.'

'It's not seven yet. How many people do you think
I'll bump into?'

'There are staff about even now. I would prefer it
if you let me go.'

Shelley began to laugh. 'Don't tell me you're old-
fashioned? How funny!'

She walked away towards the outer door of the apartment, still laughing, and didn't hear him following her
until his hand came out and stopped her just as she
was about to open the door. 'No,' he said, and that was
all.

She turned round on him, tall, slender, icily controlled. 'My, my,' she breathed, 'a masterful husband!
What are you frightened of? That somebody will fancy
me?' Her eyes sparkled. 'Or do you think I'm going to

reveal everything accidentally?' She reached up and moved the loose top of her robe slightly to one side. 'Like this?' She saw his eyes darken and change, and was filled with a heady sense of recklessness. She ran her tongue over her lips, never taking her eyes off him. 'Or *this*?' she added, and slid the gown from her thighs, showing the full length of one long slim leg. 'Have a good look,' she whispered. 'It's all *you'll* ever see!' and she turned away from him and pushed at his arm on the door. He didn't move. 'Damn you!' she breathed. 'I want to go out of here——'

'When you are dressed. Where is your key?'

'In my pocket.'

'Give it to me, please.'

'Get it yourself—lover,' she answered, and leaned against the door. He stood there for a few moments, looking down at her, and he was angry—Shelley could see that so clearly that it would have been almost frightening except for the heady knowledge she had just acquired. She did have some power to disturb him, however slight. He was angry, and a muscle moved in his dark, unshaven jaw, and as he stood there as if deciding what to do, she began to laugh.

The next moment he put his hand to the pocket on her hip and felt in it for the keys. His fingers touched briefly like fire on her side before he withdrew them with the keys and held them up. 'I'll bring you a dress,' he said. His voice was hard.

'Do. Any one from the wardrobe will do.' She moved away from the door and he went out, closing it firmly behind him. Shelley looked at it thoughtfully. A pulse of excitement beat in her throat and she smiled slowly, more of a grin than anything else, and began to walk towards the bedroom.

When he returned minutes later she called out: 'Will you put it on the bed?'

She was in the bathroom having a shower. The mirrored door was open so that she could see into the bedroom. As Vargen came in and walked over to the bed she began to soap herself, her eyes upon him for the moment he would look up—and then he did. For a long moment their eyes met, then he turned swiftly and walked out. Shelley stepped out of the shower, wrapped a towel round herself and went into the bedroom.

He had brought her a yellow cotton dress that zipped up the back. She stepped into it, pulled it up and walked into the lounge. 'Will you zip me up at the back?' she asked, and added as an afterthought: 'Please.'

He was standing by the window, looking out, and he turned, slowly. As he did, so did she, so that her back was to him. 'Mind the zipper doesn't catch,' she said softly, 'it's my bare skin.' She felt him take hold of the material, then the zip puller, and slowly ease it upwards. 'There's a little hook and eye at the top. Can you——'

'Yes, I see.' His hands were warm, a featherlight caress at the base of her neck, briefly touching her, but not deliberately.

'Thank you.' She pirouetted round. 'That better? Respectable? Can I go now—on my own—and finish dressing?'

He held out her keys and she flipped them from his hand. 'Thank you,' she said smartly. 'I'll be back in ten minutes.'

She had time to think about what had happened while she packed her case in her own suite. He did have emotions—probably only anger, but at least he wasn't totally devoid of human warmth after all. She closed her case, picked it up, and she remembered how he had looked when she had allowed him to 'accidentally' glimpse her in the shower. That hadn't been contempt or anger. It hadn't been desire either—but he hadn't been able to move for a few seconds.

Shelley smiled and went back to the penthouse. The bathroom door was closed and the shower was running. She decided to make herself another cup of coffee and went into the kitchen to do so.

Vargen emerged some half hour or so later fully dressed, shaved, his hair wet and shiny, and Shelley was reading in the lounge by the window. She looked up. 'I'm packed,' she told him. 'Oh, I forgot before.' She went over with the gift box and handed it to him. 'Thank you for the loan of the bracelet and necklace.'

He took it, frowning. 'Why are you giving me this? They are yours.' He handed the box back to her. 'It was a present.'

'You can't mean——' The words died in her throat as she saw the look in his eyes. 'A *present*?' she whispered.

'A simple gift, that was all.'

She shook her head. 'No. Really, I'd rather not. Thank you all the same, but I can't accept.'

'Why not?'

She shrugged. 'Why not? I don't know. Just because, that's all. I can't take gifts from you, and I won't. Please take the box back.'

He took it from her silently and flung it on the table, then walked away. Had she made him angry again? She sighed a little sigh. There was no way she was going to accept expensive gifts from him. Did he think she was like all his other women? If he did he would learn!

He was in the kitchen, and she followed him there. 'I

must see Walter Grey before we go,' she said.

'I will see him after breakfast. I have already phoned him.'

'I see. And then we'll set off on the yacht. How many staff are there on it?'

He looked at her in surprise. 'There are only the two of us.'

'On a large boat?'

'It's not very large, and it's easy to run.'

'But I thought——' She was confused. What *had* she thought? She hadn't actually given the subject a great deal of consideration. It had been, like the wedding, something slightly unreal. Only the wedding had taken place—and soon they would be alone, on a yacht, at sea. 'How long for?' she asked.

'Four days only.'

He was filling the kettle as he spoke, his back to her. Still angry with her? It was difficult to tell. And she didn't care anyway. Four days would soon go, and if she had to do the cooking it would be something to pass the time. 'I'll take some of those books of yours if I may,' she said.

'Of course. Whatever you wish,' he answered. No, he wasn't angry with her; he sounded totally indifferent. 'Coffee?' he said.

'Yes. Then breakfast. Can we?'

'I'll ring down for it when we've drunk this.'

'Where are we going?' she asked.

'A trip round the islands.'

She sat down at the table. 'That will be very nice.' She spoke demurely, politely, like a child being told of a visit to the zoo.

'It will be a break for me.' Vargen regarded her levelly as he handed her a cup of coffee. 'I have much to do when I return.'

'Then why go at all? I don't mind.'

He smiled, a humourless smile. 'Oh, of course,' Shelley said softly. 'Bruno would expect it, wouldn't he? Silly me! You go into partnership when we return, don't you?'

'Yes.'

'And I am free to spend my days as I wish?'

'Within reason, yes, of course.'

'I shan't be going off with other men, if that's what "within reason" means. But I'd like to see my uncle and Eileen quite a bit.'

'I didn't expect you would—but you met one yesterday——'

'Dave? The American! Good heavens, I was only having a drink——'

'It might be better if you refused any more offers like that in future. Unless of course I am with you.'

'I don't make a habit of it. He insisted—and I thought, why not? There was certainly no harm in it.'

'Others might not see it like that,' he said repressively.

'Did you?' she asked.

'No. But it was easy to see that he was attracted to you.'

She laughed. 'How observant! All right, I won't go walking alone anywhere where I'm likely to meet men. Does that suit you? I've already told you, I'll keep my part of the bargain.' She sipped her coffee. 'You might also remember that people will notice you.'

'I shall be very discreet.'

'Like you were last night? How do you know you weren't seen leaving the hotel?'

'I told you, I was working—in my office. It is down the corridor from here.'

'And I don't believe you,' she said flatly, and looked at him, her eyes cold.

He shrugged. 'It is the truth. Your opinion is your own. I can do nothing to change that.'

Shelley looked away from him. Was it the truth? She would never know. Vargen said it as though he didn't really care whether she believed him or not, which was in character. For why should he care? She meant nothing to him. She concentrated on her new resolve, and it helped. 'I'd like breakfast,' she said.

'I'll phone down for it. Excuse me.' He left her and she heard him using the telephone in the lounge, then his voice changed and she heard, 'When? Now? I see. Yes—right.' He hung up. 'Shelley!'

His voice was to be obeyed. She went out to see him standing by the telephone. He looked across the room at her, and his face was very serious. She felt her heart bump erratically for a few moments.

'What is it?' she asked.

'Your father has arrived at the airport,' he answered.

She went icily cold. 'The airport *here*—how do you know?'

'Because I contacted them last night and asked if they would let me know if a Charles Weldon arrived at any time. They telephoned the reception only minutes ago to leave the message for me. The clerk was about to ring up here when I called.'

She lifted her head proudly. 'Let him come. He can do nothing now.'

He gave a curious half smile. 'That is true. I will remain with you when he comes.' He wasn't asking her if she wanted him to, he was telling her, in a way she was glad not to have to make the decision about it herself.

'He won't be—very nice,' she said.

'I'm quite sure he won't. That is why I shall stay.'

It would take him about half an hour, allowing for the brief Customs check, and finding a taxi. He must be extremely angry to have left his business and flown out here. Shelley sat down. 'I don't think I'm hungry,' she said.

'Yes, you will eat. We will be up here having our breakfast when he arrives—do you understand, child? What could be more natural?'

She looked at him again. He was right of course, as always. There would be a sense of unity, the two of them sitting together at a table when her father arrived, and he would undoubtedly be well aware of it. 'Yes, I see,' she answered.

'It's on its way up. Go and get yourself ready.'

'Ready?' She looked blankly at him. He had called her a child. At the moment she felt like one, entirely in his hands.

Vargen gave a little smile. 'Don't women feel better when they have lipstick and perfume on?'

Shelley nodded. 'I suppose so.' She had to pass near him to get her make-up bag, and she felt the nearness of him, the hard strength of him like warm vibrations that surrounded her. She looked at him and gave a little smile, hesitating as she was about to pass him. 'I'm not really frightened,' she said. 'Not any more. Thanks for that.' He didn't make any attempt to touch her, but it was as though he had. The look he gave her was enough. His tawny gold eyes were upon her as he said softly:

'Perhaps you are already free of him.'

'Am I? I don't know.' She gave a little shiver, and her eyes were caught by his so that she couldn't look away. Of course—she had nearly forgotten that Vargen knew her father. That, in a way, was another battle, nothing to do with her. Nothing was clear-cut and simple, if it ever had been; it was a complex situation, yet she was a part of it now because she was Vargen's wife, even if it was in name only. She sensed his tremendous strength and knew that now, at last, her father would meet his match. She made a small, wordless sound of pain, and Vargen moved.

He moved towards her, and it seemed to be happening in slow motion, for he was only a foot or so away and yet it was as if he took ages to reach her, as if the air shimmered with sound and colour as his arms came out to hold her arms. Shelley felt the trembling begin inside her so that he must feel it, but it no longer mattered because she wanted him so much to touch her, to hold her, to take her in his arms and never let go. . . .

'Yes,' he said, oh, so very quietly, 'I think you are free. You are safe with me.'

'I know.' A teardrop trembled on her lower lashes, and her eyes were wide. 'Why? I don't understand why —I mean, this is a business arrangement for you. You don't even have to see him if you don't want—I know how you feel about everything——'

'Because I have told you—but what you don't know is that I would not see anyone suffer.'

'You? When nothing means much to you except money?' She tried a laugh, but failed. Her heart was beating too fast for comfort. What was it she saw in his eyes?

'Not strictly true.' His smile reached his eyes. They weren't hard any more.

'I don't understand you.' And I never will, she added mentally.

'No one does. Accept what I say.'

'I have to. There's not much time, is there?'

'No. Soon he will be here—and soon also will our

breakfast, I think.' Then he did something very strange. He moved his hands up and cupped her face in them. 'Trust me, Shelley. When we go to the boat this morning it will sever the ties finally with your father. He cannot stop us, whatever he thinks—and then he will know you are free.'

She trembled at his touch. His hands were so strong, but they could be gentle too, as she was finding now. She had completely forgotten that she had told him never to touch her. 'Yes,' she whispered.

There was a discreet rattle of crockery outside the door and a pause before the knock came. Vargen moved away and the shimmering spell was broken.

'Come in,' he called.

Two waiters came in with a loaded trolley and began to push it over to the table at the far end of the large room. 'We'll serve ourselves,' said Vargen.

'As you wish, sir.' The head waiter bowed to them both and clicked his fingers for his assistant. 'Come, Mario.'

They were alone again. Shelley walked over, took the dazzling white cloth from the trolley drawer and laid it over the table. Vargen followed, and pushed the trolley the last few yards. There was a veritable cornucopea; croissants, butter, apricot jam, fresh orange juice in a glass jug, clinking with ice, fresh fruits in a dish, slivers of sweet ham, and avocado pears. And underneath, a silver coffee pot, cream, china cups and saucers. She noticed that there were three cups.

'Sit, and we will eat,' said Vargen.

Shelley sat down. It seemed that if she did exactly as he said, all would be well. She poured herself coffee, took an avocado pear and a little ham and began eating. The telephone shrilled at the other end of the room. He looked at her as he got up.

'It could be him,' he said.

It was. She listened as he instructed that someone bring her father up, then replaced the receiver. He walked back across the room, sat down, took a croissant and buttered it. It was still hot, and the butter melted as he put it on. Shelley watched it in fascination, trying to ignore the spreading numbness that seemed to be filling her. In another minute. . . .

There was a knock at the door, the reception clerk's voice: 'Mr Gilev, sir.'

'Come in,' he answered, and the door opened and her father walked in. Instantly the room was filled with his anger. It hit Shelley like a wave, and she stood up.

'Father——' she began.

He looked at her, then turned to Vargen. 'So it *is* you,' he said. Vargen had left the table and gone across to meet him. Neither man held out a hand, which didn't surprise Shelley in the least. The hostility that filled the room could have been cut with a knife.

'Yes, it is I,' replied Vargen. 'We meet again Mr Weldon. As you see, we are breakfasting. Will you join us?'

'I've come to take Shelley home,' said Charles Weldon, addressing her for the first time. 'Get your cases.'

'I'm about to go on my honeymoon, Father,' she told him, surprised at how steady her voice sounded.

He laughed, 'Honeymoon? With this?' He cocked a contemptuous thumb in Vargen's direction. 'Good God, woman, don't you know why he's married you? I'll tell you.' His hard blue eyes were blazing with the rage he was barely keeping under control.

'I already know,' she said quickly. 'But there's nothing you can do about it. We're legally married.'

'Nothing I can do?' He strode across the room to the table she stood by. 'Nothing?' He took hold of her arm. 'You'll see what I *can* do! I'm taking you back to England——'

She tried to pull her arm free, but his grip was like a vice, and immediately all her fears rushed back as she trembled in his grip. There had been too many times, not only the occasion she had told Vargen about, when Charles Weldon had beaten her that the memories excluded everything else, even the presence of Vargen. And her father was an exceptionally strong and tough man, a keep-fit fanatic who had been a very good amateur boxer and still practised regularly.

'Please——' she began.

'Let my wife go,' said Vargen, and Charles Weldon looked round contemptuously.

'Just keep out of this, Gilev,' he snapped. 'It no longer concerns you. And after today she'll not be your wife——'

Vargen moved swiftly and quietly towards them, reached out to her father's arm and applied pressure on it. She was free. Shelley pulled away, rubbing the forearm where her father had gripped, and looked at him and began to cry out——

He could move swiftly too. He turned round and swung a punch at the younger man—but Vargen had moved back and the punch never landed.

'I don't want to fight you,' he said.

'Because you're a bloody coward,' Charles Weldon snarled. 'Well, I'm going to give you a hiding you won't forget, and when I've finished with you I'm leaving with *my* daughter——'

'No, you're not. I'm so sorry, but you're——'

Her father launched himself forward, and there was

a loud crack—Shelley closed her eyes, unable to stand it any longer. Then silence, a groan, and a thud. She opened her eyes.

Vargen was helping her father to his feet. 'Listen to me,' he said. 'You cannot fight me. Believe me, I have no wish to, but I *will* defend myself, do I make myself clear? Don't try to touch me again—instead, we will talk.' He pushed him into a chair and said to Shelley, 'Go into the bedroom and wait.'

'But——' she began, and Vargen looked at her. She was silenced.

'Please go now,' he said. 'It is all right.'

Her father looked dazed. He looked as if all the wind had been knocked out of him, and he wasn't ready to speak.

She walked quietly past them into the bedroom, and over to the window. She heard Vargen beginning to talk. His voice was quiet, and she couldn't distinguish the words, but she sensed the force behind them. There was no sound from her father. None at all, not yet.

She went and closed the door, then sat on the bed, prepared to wait. There seemed nothing else she could do. Vargen had effectively taken control of the situation. She looked down at her hands and they were steadier now. All she had to do was wait.

CHAPTER SEVEN

THE sun blazed down on to the deck. Shelley sat in the comparative shade, in a lounging chair, looking out at the fast receding island of Avala. Vargen was at the controls, and they were alone, and would be for the next four days.

The man they had left behind at the hotel was a different man from the father she had known for the last twenty-three years. His anger had changed into a kind of smouldering acceptance. He wasn't happy—would he ever be?—but whatever Vargen and he had talked about, and the conversation in the lounge had taken a good half hour, something had worked. He would never forgive her for getting married, for 'escaping' from his dominance, but at least he was no longer threatening. Vargen hadn't told her what had been said, and she wouldn't ask, but the balance was altered, and the threats were no longer in evidence when she had at last returned to them. Her father had looked up at her and she had seen the dislike in his eyes. He didn't attempt to conceal that. And there had been something else.

'You've made your mind up,' he had said, 'and you've chosen your life—and that's an end to it. Don't expect my blessings, because you won't get them. And when I leave here, we won't see each other again—I hope that's clear?'

Shelley nodded, dry-eyed. So that was it—and yet only what she had known all along. She had expected to feel shattered at his words, but all she felt was a sensation of relief. 'I know,' she had answered. 'I'm sorry, but if that's the way you feel——' and she had turned away and gone to the window.

Then he had gone. Her life had changed irrevocably in that hour while he had been there, and when he had left something had gone with him. And she was free.

She sat up now, and looked at the island; it was a misty smudge, no more, and she felt very alone. At least, there, there had been other people.

Immediately her father had left Vargen had changed. He might have been a stranger again, the one she didn't understand. He had looked at her.

'How soon can you be ready to leave?' he had asked.

'I'm ready now,' she had answered. Dry-eyed, she had looked at him. What was it? He was once again the hard-eyed, hard-faced man, the stranger who had married her for his own selfish reasons. It was as though a wall had been erected between them, and she had stared at him, searching for any sign of softening. There was none.

'Then soon we leave.' He had walked away from her then, picked up the telephone and told the staff he would be ready to leave in half an hour.

'I'm going to my office,' he had told her. 'I will return, then we will leave.' He had gone out.

Between that time and now, as she sat on the sunny deck, not more than a dozen words had been exchanged. Vargen had taken her aboard and carried her luggage to a small comfortable cabin with a double bed, a wardrobe and built-in cupboards, and her own minuscule shower and toilet. 'This is your room,' he said, 'mine is two cabins along. Feel free to do as you wish.'

He had gone, and a few minutes later had come the deep throb of the engines starting up, the sense of movement, at first gradual, a shifting round, then the steady hum of the motors, and the island receding through her porthole.

Shelley had put on a trim black swimsuit, gone up on deck, found the lounging chair, and sat on it. She had lain back for a few minutes and then watched Avala receding.

Now she looked at her watch. It was gone eleven. She hadn't seen round the yacht, but it was compact, with a fair sized deck, a hatchway to the cabins below, and the control room up a ladder, above her. A low white rail surrounded the deck, with lifebelts hung at intervals, with the yacht's name emblazoned on in white on a red strip: *Helena*. The lines of the yacht were graceful and sleek, it cut through the water swiftly and smoothly, and she didn't know or care where they were going.

She stood up. All round her the sea, no land in sight. She went over to the rails and leaned over, seeing the clean white spray cut by the boat, and a gull skimming the water in search of food. She was thirsty. She wasn't hungry, even though she had eaten little that morning, but she needed a drink. She made her way down the narrow wooden stairs and into the passage. Five doors led off. Hers was the first on the right. She opened the door on the left to see a small lounge. The next door led to the galley and she went in. There was a cooker on gimbals, a large refrigerator, and several white fitted cupboards. There was also a large sink and draining board, a fixed table and two benches. She began to open cupboards. All the cups and plates were secured; she took out a glass, opened the refrigerator to see it crammed with food, fresh milk, bottles of orange juice, fruit, and, in the freezer, packs of frozen meat and fish. She poured out a glass of milk and drank it slowly. And now what? She should see if Vargen needed a drink, and if she should prepare lunch. But she didn't want to. He would be at the controls all the time, she imagined, for a boat couldn't steer itself—or could it? She wasn't sure. And if that were the case, she might see very little of him.

As she sat down to think about it, she felt the motors slowing, become less even, the engine note changing and deepening as the boat gradually slowed down. There was a rattling sound, a deep heavy rattling, then silence.

She waited, puzzled, and heard his footsteps on the stairs. The next moment he stood in the doorway and looked at her. He wore only trousers. She had seen him half naked before, when he had been asleep, when he had been completely relaxed. Now he was tense as a coiled spring, his muscles hard, as hard as him.

'We've stopped?' she asked. For a moment she wasn't sure if he would bother to answer.

'Yes.' He came in, opened the refrigerator and took out a bottle of orange juice. 'We'll eat soon, then you can look round the island.'

'What island?'

'The one I've stopped near.' He swallowed the juice and put his cup in the sink. He looked at her, his eyes cool and hard. 'You can swim ashore.'

She didn't know why he had changed. Surely he didn't blame her for her father's behaviour? Perhaps she was seeing him as he really was. Whatever the reason, she didn't like it, and she didn't at that moment like him.

'*I* can?' she said quietly. 'Aren't *you* going?'

His eyes raked her face. 'I'll see. I don't know.'

'Well, don't stop on my account,' she retorted. 'Don't feel you have to entertain me. You've made it clear enough already what a big bore you find this whole honeymoon, and quite frankly, so do I!' She glared back at him, her temper rising fast. 'So let's not pretend. We're alone now, remember? We don't have Bruno here to impress.' She laughed. 'I'll sit and read on deck and you can just do precisely what you like. Now tell me what I'm to make for lunch and I'll do it.'

'Anything—I don't mind.'

'Right.' She went over to the refrigerator, reached out the first pack of meat from the freezer and banged it down on the draining board. 'I'll get on with this.' She turned to him. 'I'll call you when it's ready.'

He walked out without another word, and she watched him go. Then she unwrapped the meat, two succulent steaks, and put them under the grill while she looked out vegetables to go with them. Damn him, she muttered to herself, filling a pan with water, and throwing in beans and potatoes. Let him cook if he didn't like her way. She just didn't care any more. He was hateful!

She made herself coffee while she waited for the vegetables to cook. She didn't know where Vargen was, and she didn't care any more. He was loathesome! He was —she looked at the porthole which was wide open, and blinked. He was—hard, cold, hurtful. And the awful thing was, she didn't know why. He had never been like this before, not this bad, not like this. She didn't realise then, not until much later, why.

She went ashore to the small uninhabited island an hour after they had eaten lunch. Vargen had dropped anchor in a sheltered bay, and she had only to climb down the ladder and swim a few dozen yards before feeling the smooth sand beneath her. She left Vargen preparing his fishing lines aboard the yacht. Preoccupied, he hadn't even looked up when she told him she was going,

merely nodded as if it were not the slightest interest to
him.

She walked along the beach. Lush palm trees grew
to her right, and the air was sweet with the scent of
colourful wild flowers, most of which she didn't recognise. Some were like orchids, curling themselves around
the branches of the trees, and the leaves rustled in a
slight, cooling breeze. Now at last alone, she had time
to think clearly. She walked until she had rounded a
curve and the yacht was hidden, and there she sat down
on the hot dry sand, littered with tiny shells and dried
seaweed, and leaned her back against a tree. The bark
was hard, and faintly prickly. She looked out to sea. It
shimmered in the sun, the horizon a dark clear line
curving faintly away to infinity.

Where she sat was not in the direct sunlight, but it
was still very hot. Shelley closed her eyes. Her swim-
suit was already dry on her, and the sand clung to her
legs, a powdery gold. Soon she would explore the
island, which was only small. How wonderful it would
be to be here with a man she loved—and who loved her.
She gave a slight bitter smile. Instead of which she was
here with a stranger. It wasn't her imagination: Vargen
had changed since that morning. Since breakfast, in
fact—and since her father's arrival. It was hard to
think clearly in the intense heat, but it seemed important for her to do so. On board, knowing he was
near, thought was even more difficult in the stifling
atmosphere, but here on the island she was sufficiently
alone to be free of it.

The two men had spoken for a long time. At first
Vargen had done most of the talking—but then she
had heard both men's voices. So her father, after the
first initial shock, would have rallied his defences. And
he was clever, no doubt about that. So what could he

have said to Vargen to make him change? Then slowly, oh, so slowly, there came into Shelley's mind the realisation of what it could have been—and what was, with her father, infinitely possible.

'Oh, God!' she murmured softly, as the idea became clearer and more rooted. It would suit her father's twisted mind—it might even give him a certain satisfaction, if he thought Vargen loved her—and, not knowing of their strange arrangement, that would be what he was forced to think—oh, yes, it would satisfy him greatly to tell Vargen that she was promiscuous—and it would be just the sort of thing he would, and could do. Subtly too, not chancing another blow from a younger, stronger man. Oh, no, he'd be very clever, the way he did it, the words he chose....

She took a deep shuddering breath. It fitted, it all fitted. The tiny light of triumph she had seen in her father's eyes when he left. The light of sheer satisfied spite that she hadn't understood because too many things had been happening all at once.... But then, even if Vargen believed, why would he care? He wouldn't of course, why should he? She meant nothing to him, save as an attractive accessory to give *him* respectability for Bruno's—and the partnership's—sake. And he had no room to talk about anyone's morals in any case.

Shelley sat forward and begun brushing sand from her legs. She needed some physical activity, if only that, for she was experiencing a sense of welling anger within her. *If* she was right—and she was already making up her mind to find out, one way or another, how, she hadn't decided, then the one big question remained. Why should Vargen have changed so much?

She stood up and began to walk further round the island. The air shimmered in the heat, the sand seem-

ing to dance beneath her feet and around her, and the
sea sparkled in millions of dancing diamond points
that dazzled her eyes. She had to tread carefully to avoid
the many shells—some quite sharp-edged, underfoot,
and it helped her to concentrate her thoughts.

Gradually she worked out a logical reason in her
mind for Vargen's behaviour. It was absurd, but it was
the only theory she had, and the more she thought
about it the more sense it began to make. What was it
he had said to her when he had first made his bizarre
proposition? She tried to remember the exact words,
but couldn't. The gist of them was that she had an air
of innocence about her, that she didn't look sexually
experienced—he had even asked her if she were a
virgin. She remembered that, and her own indigna-
tion at the personal question. She felt her mouth
tighten as the anger came back more sharply. Of
course! It was the usual male conceit—the sheer arrogance—the always having to be right. How well she
knew that, with her father, over the years. Vargen
would be shocked to have been 'fooled', as he must
have regarded it.

Shelley began to smile, and the smile rippled into
laughter as she began to see a funny side to it all. Better
to laugh than to cry. And there was a *funny* side. Because if she was right, and her father had managed to
give Vargen the impression that he had married a
swinger, and Vargen believed it and was perturbed by
it, she was going to turn it to her advantage. She wasn't
sure how, yet, but there would certainly be time to
work on it. Time was something she had a lot of. Yet
if only he knew the truth! No man had ever made love
to her, the main reason being that she had never met
any man who attracted her sufficiently—before Vargen.
And that was even funnier, because there had been that

moment after the kiss when she would have given herself to him completely.... But he certainly would never
know that, not now.

She was now on the other side of the small island,
and away from the boat, from which Vargen was probably fishing. Shelley paused in the shelter of a large
shady palm tree, studying the shells that abounded. She
crouched down, and a tiny crab scuttered away towards
the water. Carefully she sat down, watching its progress,
the sideways walk of it, quickly, towards the shelter and
protection of its home, the sea. An inquisitive gull
landed several feet away and looked at her, head tilted
as if debating whether or not she would have any tit-
bits. The beady yellow eye regarded her unsmilingly
and she stared back at it. 'Sorry,' she said. 'No food,'
and it took off with a loud shriek as if it understood.

The crab was nearly in the sea now—then it was
covered by water, and a few tiny bubbles rose, and the
sea had swallowed it up. Shelley thought about the little
crab, with its hard shell to protect it from attack. A
hard shell....

That's what I need, she thought. For protection—
from love. Vargen didn't need a hard shell, because he
was hard enough, but I'm not, she thought—only I'm
going to learn, to build a wall round me, then I'll be
safe too.

It was time to go, to see if her theory was right after
all. As she walked slowly back to the yacht she began
to make plans in her mind; unformed as yet, mere ideas,
but gathering shape with every step she took.

She rounded the curve, and it was there, dazzling
white, riding at anchor and bobbing gently in the
waves. Vargen sat on deck, changed into denim shorts
that were very brief. He held a fishing rod, and he wore
a denim Beatle-type cap on his head, and had a cheroot

in his mouth. He looked like an advertisement for cigars, Shelley thought wryly. A man without a care in the world—apparently. That thought made her laugh too, and he heard, and looked up, and she saw the slight movement of his head in the distance and looked steadily back at him, uncaring.

She walked slowly towards him, and when she reached a point where it became easier to swim than continue along the beach, she walked into the sea and began swimming with leisurely strokes, revelling in the salty buoyancy. She reached the fixed ladder and climbed up over the rail and on to the deck. Vargen looked round, seemed about to look away again, then frowned. His eyes were on her feet, and Shelley looked down. She could see nothing untoward. Two feet, two legs, that was all.

'Your foot,' he said.

'So?' she looked up at him. He didn't know that she knew. It was like having a little secret.

'Look behind you,' he said dryly, and stood up as he spoke, wedging the rod at an angle between the cross rails. Shelley did so, saw the small spots of blood on the deck, and lifted her right foot. Blood oozed from the sole, and she remembered the slight pricking feeling she had had just before going into the water.

'You'd better stay there. I'll get a plaster,' he said, and walked past her to the steps down to the cabins.

He didn't want his deck messed up. She couldn't blame him for that, so she stood patiently in the blazing sun until she heard him returning.

'Sit on the lounger,' he said. He was carrying a large grey steel box with a large red cross painted on a white circle.

'I'll do it,' she said.

'Don't be silly,' he answered. Shelley put her tongue

out at his retreating back and followed him to the
lounger.

When she was seated she held up her foot, and the
blood dripped down on to the deck. 'Dear me,' she said.
'A good job there were no sharks near!'

He didn't answer. He knelt and opened the box and
began lifting out scissors, box of plaster dressings,
bottle of antiseptic lotion, cotton wool. She watched
him, her mind cool and analytical. What was going on
in his mind? It would be interesting to find out.

He applied lotion to a wad of cotton wool and, holding her foot up at the ankle, began to clean the cut,
eyes narrowed, concentrating. Then he looked up.
'You've a bit of shell still in,' he said. 'It needs to come
out.'

'I can't feel anything,' she began.

'You would if I left it. Stay right there I'll go and
fetch the tweezers.' He hurried and went down the
steps again. Shelley sat back in the lounger, making
herself more comfortable, and waited. He was being
civil, no more; she would do the same to him if he cut
his foot. She watched him returning a few minutes later.
He had good legs, as tanned and hard as the rest of him.
Long legs, muscular thighs, granite hard, powerful....
She looked away, feigning interest in the state of her
foot. He had the legs of an athlete and she wondered
why she should suddenly feel dizzy.

'This may hurt a little,' he said, and his eyes met hers,
and they were giving nothing away. A stranger's eyes,
cold and hard.

'I'll live,' she said, and smiled at him, because she
knew something he didn't, and she felt almost good
about it. She was beginning to build the shell around
her, and soon he wouldn't be able to hurt her at all, but
he didn't know that either.

He knelt without answering, held her foot again, and very carefully put the tweezers to the sole. She gritted her teeth, determined that whatever happened she wouldn't make a sound. There was a sharp, brief, stabbing pain, and it was all over. Vargen held up the tweezers and she saw the small sliver of shell, covered with blood, gripped at the points of the tweezers. 'That's it,' he said.

'Thank you.' He flung the piece over the side, applied more antiseptic, and found a broad square of plaster dressing and placed it on her foot.

'Now try and stand,' he said. She did so.

'It's all right,' she told him. 'A little sore, that's all. I honestly didn't feel a thing before, and I was walking carefully to avoid the shells.'

He shrugged. 'It's easily done. Now I will return to my fishing.'

'And I shall sunbathe.'

Shelley went down to her cabin, took the bottle of suntan oil from her dressing table, then paused. She hadn't yet unpacked her case. She went over to it, put it on the bed and opened it, feeling inside. She smiled a little to herself as she pulled out two strips of red cloth and held them up. Then she pulled off her swim-suit and began to put on the bikini pants. Walking across to the mirror, she surveyed herself for a moment or two. The bikini pants were extremely brief, a mere triangle of nylon with red strips at the side. She had a good figure, hips rounded but not too full, long slender legs. She stood up straight and tall, looked at her breasts, then carefully fastened on the top, adjusting the fit to accentuate the cleavage. She had bought the bikini on an impulse, and never worn it before, but because it took up no more room than a couple of handkerchiefs had popped it in her case, and now she was pleased that she had. It was after all, only what Vargen would expect her to wear—if her theory was right. She turned sideways, well satisfied with the profile presented in the mirror. She had never thought much about her figure before, but then she had never been married to a man like Vargen Gilev before, and she had a few weapons of her own, and she was going to use them.

She picked up the bottle of oil and went up on to the deck. Vargen had his back to her and didn't move or look round. Shelley crossed to the lounger, adjusted it so that it was flat, like a bed, and sat on it while she smoothed on the oil all over her skin not covered by the minuscule pieces of cloth. Then she lay down on her back and closed her eyes.

Fifteen minutes or so later she turned over. As she did so, she took off the bikini top then lay face down. Soon—not just yet. It had to be timed carefully, casually.... Ten minutes later she called: 'Vargen?'

'Yes?'

'Are you thirsty?'

'Yes. Are you?' She chanced a brief look at him from half-closed eyes. He still hadn't looked round. He hadn't caught any fish either. Perhaps they'd seen him coming and fled.

'Yes. Shall I get us a drink?'

She saw him move and closed her eyes quickly. 'No, I will go.'

'Thank you.' She stayed with her eyes closed until she heard him clattering barefoot down the wooden steps. Then she let her breath out in a long sigh. Any time now....

She heard him coming up again, slowly, and raised herself on her elbows, her left arm in front of her as though trying to conceal her nakedness. A quick glance

down confirmed that she hadn't quite succeeded—
which was precisely the effect she planned.

She looked up and watched him emerge round the
corner and she watched his eyes. He faltered, for a
second only, but it was enough. He carried two tall
glasses full of orange juice, and the ice clinked in them
and he seemed to be holding them very tightly, but that
might have been her imagination. She smiled brightly.
'Thanks,' she said, and reached out her right hand and
made an ineffectual attempt to appear modest, looking
down shyly. Vargen handed her a glass, saying nothing.

'Have you caught anything?' she asked.

'No.'

'Oh dear,' she said, and she moved slightly, and he
turned away. She watched him go to the rail, but he
didn't sit down again. He stood there looking out to
the island while he drank his fruit juice. His back was
very eloquent. It was a very dignified back—and an
angry one. Shelley didn't know how she knew he was
angry, but she did. She buried her face in the pillow
and smothered a laugh. She'd only just begun, but he
wasn't to know that. She had never thought that it
could be possible to love and hate a person all at the
same time, but now she knew it was. The part of her
that loved him wanted to touch him, to love and be
loved by him, and the hating part wanted to hurt him,
to make him suffer as she had suffered, and the feelings
all mingled, and she knew she had to separate them,
which was difficult. She watched him. He had finished
the drink, and emptied the ice over the side.

'Can I go swimming?' she called.

'If you wish.' His voice was harsh and deep. 'As long
as you stay by the boat.'

'Of course.' She sat up. She knew he wouldn't look
round, and he didn't. She put on the bikini top and

went to the ladder, stepping down carefully, avoiding direct contact with the sore part of her foot. The water felt cool in contrast with the burning sun, and she slid into it with a little sigh of pleasure. It was balm to the skin, like moving around in dark green satin, smooth and caressing. She swam around the other side of the boat and turned on her back, kicking lazily to propel herself along. The water lapped over her face, tingling her skin. It was so easy just to float. There was no current, or at least none she could feel, and the water was buoyant and clean and clear. She had no idea of the time although the sun had now left the top of the sky and was moving towards the distant horizon. There was silence, an utter, beautiful nothingness....

Then sudden nightmare gripping her legs so that she couldn't move, and she panicked, head going under as the cramp struck her, so that she came up gasping and spluttering, looked for the boat. It was too far; she had floated further than she realised. Shelley cried out something, she wasn't sure what, and began to swim, using her arms only, her legs useless, and saw Vargen looking out towards her over the rail, tilting his arm, shouting something, and in that awful moment she thought she was going to drown, and wondered if he was unable to swim. Because if he could, surely he would have been in the water before now? The sea caught her roughly, swamping her, and she gasped and tried to turn over, to float, but she swallowed water, felt her head fill with it, dark green, in her eyes, and ears, and nose....

She seemed to hear in the midst of the nightmare a distant splash, but she was concentrating on trying to keep alive and that was the most important thing, to keep alive.

She was grabbed, head held, and she drew in a desperate shuddering breath and heard Vargen's voice in her ear, rough, commanding: 'Stay still, do not struggle,' then she felt his arm supporting her round her body, and now she was safe. She obeyed his urgent commands and was towed along slowly but surely towards the boat, nearer, ever nearer.

'Cramp in my legs,' she managed to whisper.

'Be quiet. Don't talk,' he ordered, and she was silent, eyes open, seeing the sky spiralling round, the points of light flashing in her head, tasting the salt water, gagging on it.

Then a bump, and he hauled her over his shoulder and thus up the steps on to the deck where he laid her face down. She felt the pressure of his hard hands on her back and gasped, gushing out sea-water, feeling suddenly sick. She tried to protest, but it came out as a croak, and she felt the ruthless hands—then merciful release. They stopped, and he turned her over and picked her up and carried her over to the lounger.

'You *fool*! You stupid bloody *fool*!' he raged, and it wasn't quite true, what he had said before, that he rarely lost his temper, because this was a monumental rage, and he trembled with it, and she knew that if she had been a man he would very probably have hauled her up and beaten her. Only she wasn't and he couldn't but the feeling was there so strongly that she cringed.

Then he did. He caught her arms and pulled her up until she was standing—trembling too—and shook her. 'I told you to stay near the boat!' he grated, every word emphasised, staccato.

'I—I'm sorry——' she could scarcely speak. 'It—it didn't seem as if I——'

'Be quiet!' He let go of her arms so suddenly that she nearly overbalanced, and turned away from her as if he couldn't bear to touch her. Shelley sank down on to the lounger on weakened legs, the cramplike pains still an agony to her muscles. She let out her breath in a shuddering sigh, her arms bruised from the steely grip, and watched as Vargen strode over to the rail and jerked in his fishing rod as though he would like to break it in two. Then he flung it on the deck and turned to her again.

'Go down to your cabin,' he ordered, 'and change.'

The first shocks were passing. She was still weak, but recovering fast. All right, so he had saved her life, and he was angry, as he had a right to be, but it didn't mean he could order her about like some naughty child. She glared at him. 'No, I won't!' she retorted. 'I'm sunbathing.'

'We are leaving here. You have sunbathed long enough. The next thing you'll have a sunstroke, and I can scarcely rescue you from that,' he snapped.

'Don't talk so big with me,' she snapped back. 'I'm not your *servant*!'

'You are my wife——'

'Hah! Big deal! We all know what that means! Go and take a running jump at yourself, big boy,' she said scornfully, turned her back on him, and very deliberately and carefully sat down on the lounger, then looked at him. 'I'm staying here,' she said. 'So what are you going to do about that?' And she made the mistake of trying a mocking smile.

That was only the first mistake. She made the second one a few seconds later when he strode over and pulled her up again, and she fought furiously to free herself, kicking and pummelling. Vargen took both her hands in his right one, held them tightly together so that she was securely imprisoned, leaned down, swept her off her feet with his left arm and carried her, shouting and writhing vainly, down the steps to her cabin. Inside he kicked the door with his foot and dragged her to her case, and with the free hand opened it, searched, pulled out a yellow cotton dress, and said:

'You have the choice. Either you change—or I'll do it for you.'

Their eyes met. He meant it, every word. Shelley saw the hard anger in his eyes, saw the set of his face, the lines of his mouth, and knew he would do precisely that. A wave of something like excitement rushed through her, a tingling in the bones, a pounding under her skin, and she felt the pulse beating at her throat, nearly choking her. Now, soon, she might know if all her wild imaginings had been right or not.

She smiled, slowly, secretly. 'You wouldn't dare,' she whispered, and her heart thudded in her breast, and she thought she might faint.

Vargen moved, so swiftly that she was scarcely aware, she had no time to catch her breath, to say she had changed her mind, she didn't mean it. He moved, and the next moment she was naked.

CHAPTER EIGHT

Suddenly it was not what she had wanted. Shelley grabbed the bath towel from the bed and whipped it round her. 'You beast!' she whispered, voice shaking. 'You *beast*——'

'Yes. Am I not? Put on the dress.'

'I'll see you in hell first!' Her eyes flashed fire. The pounding excitement still filled her, but it was mixed with anger at his sheer arrogance. 'Just get out of here —get out!'

He looked down at her body, scarcely covered by the towel, his eyes raking the length of her, and then slowly he raised his eyes to her face again and was very still.

'Seen enough?' she whispered. She held his glance boldly. She wasn't going to look away first. She lifted her chin defiantly and her eyes blazed her temper. 'Nothing to say?' she taunted. 'That's a change!'

'So innocent,' he murmured softly. 'So very innocent——'

Then she knew. She knew that she was right. It all fell into place now. She could almost have told him what her father had said about her. Although Vargen's words were softly spoken, they held more anger and contempt than if he had shouted or stormed.

'That's why you married me, isn't it?' she mocked. 'For my innocent air? And—oh yes, *class*. My air of class and respectability.' She swung away from him, allowing the towel to fall slightly, and laughed. 'And here I am. All yours—for the next six months, every *innocent* inch of me. All right, you go now. I'll get my clothes on like a good girl.' He didn't move, so she continued: 'Unless you want to stay and watch—husband?'

Without a word he walked out. Shelley watched him go and then sank slowly on to the bed. 'Phew!' She wasn't sure what had happened, but it had been pretty explosive. And she didn't have to guess any more. At least now she knew. She stood up and carried the yellow dress over to her wardrobe and hung it up. She was going to wear something else. Perfectly respectable, but— she gave a grin and searched out two innocent garments, brief shorts, and red vest-type sun-top. She held up the top, then slipped it over her head and surveyed the effect in the mirror. Vargen couldn't do much about that. Or could he? It provided adequate covering— for a beach at least. They were seen all the time. She pulled on pants, and the shorts, zipped them up, and took another look. The effect, she was pleased to note, was slightly more devastating than the bikini. She marched out of the door, fully recovered, and went up on deck. There was no sign of Vargen, but she could hear him moving about in the control room ahead and slightly above her. She went up the ladder and peeped in.

'All right?' she asked. 'Will this suffice, oh, master?'

He was busy at the control panel and didn't answer or look round, so she waited just inside the doorway. It was a very small cabin, scarcely room to move round, but beautifully equipped. There was a wheel, a compass, radio, dozens of dials and switches in a dazzling —and puzzling—array. From this vantage point could be seen a panoramic view practically all round the yacht.

Vargen was engaged with some complicated-looking

mechanism, and she heard a low distant clanking and turmoil that vibrated beneath them, and realised he was hauling up the anchor.

Then silence. He turned. 'We are leaving now. Go down below.' He glanced only briefly at her, then turned away again.

Shelley pulled a face at his back. 'How long will you be up here?'

'For as long as we travel.'

'What about food?' she queried.

'I will eat when we anchor for the night, not before. Do as you wish—eat when you like.'

'Very well. Don't you want a drink?'

'No, I can have a can of beer. That will suffice.'

That seemed to be the end of the conversation, and Shelley, sensing his total preoccupation, turned and went down the steps. How easily he could change, from raging temper to coolness within minutes, while she was still in a turmoil.

She looked around her on deck. So much for grand gestures of defiance! He had scarcely noticed her. And now what? His remarks about sunbathing had been sensible, although she wouldn't have admitted it to him. Until her skin was used to the sun, she would be foolish to stay in it for too long a period. She went down to her cabin, unpacked her clothes, then decided to look around the yacht.

Besides her own cabin there was the galley, the small saloon, Vargen's cabin—identical to her own, except that his bed was larger, and another smaller cabin with two bunk beds. So the yacht could sleep six in comfort, she thought. She explored the galley more fully, then went into the saloon she had only briefly glimpsed before. A long low seat ran along the outer wall, covered in dark brown flower-patterned material. The floor was

thickly carpeted in a toning brown carpet, and there
was a dining table of rich dark wood, secured to the
floor. Drawers in the table revealed exquisite cutlery.
There was a sideboard, a wall cupboard in the same
dark wood, and six matched chairs. The walls were
cream, and there were three paintings on the walls of
the saloon, and instead of portholes were large picture
windows which let in the sunlight, flooding in through
the partly drawn curtains. Shelley drew them back
fully, and the pictures emerged in their full glory.
There were two of Turner's magnificent sea pictures—
what else? she thought wryly—and the third was a portrait of a woman, head and shoulders only; the woman
was beautiful, dark-haired, with deep amber eyes and
high cheekbones, and a full sensuous mouth. Shelley
studied the picture for several minutes, appreciating
the delicacy of the brush-strokes as well as the subject.
A lot of love had gone into that painting. Whoever had
done it wasn't a first-rate artist, but any deficiencies
were unimportant because what emerged was a feeling
of satisfaction in the viewer of it at such a complete
picture. Shelley found it fascinating. There was something written in the bottom right-hand corner, so small
that it was difficult to read it, but she stood on tiptoe to
peer, and made out the word 'Helena'.

Then she stepped back past the table to see it in
perspective. This then was the woman the boat had
been named after, and the only question was—who was
she? Vargen had only ever loved one woman—so he
had said—and it was unlikely to be her after what had
happened. Shelley turned away, vaguely disturbed and
curious, and, for something to do, to stop the confusing
thoughts that clamoured in her brain, opened the wall
cupboard to see what was inside. That was the second
surprise. It was full of painting equipment; canvases,

brushes, a folding easel, boxes of oil and water and poster paints all secured and fastened in with thick cords. Shelley managed to lift out several canvases. Three were new, unused, three had sketches in charcoal on, one scene clearly from the beach at Avala, another a rough attempt at a fisherman sitting by his boat—and the third——

She put the canvases down on the table carefully. They were all stretched on to wooden frames, and made a hollow sound as she put them down and stared at the third, which was of a child. Although it was only a rough sketch, it was so vivid that it seemed to leap from the canvas at her. A little girl, possibly three or four, with curly hair, large eyes, a smiling mouth, standing holding a doll, dressed in a simple shift dress, and there was no great detail. It was as though it had been done quickly, to capture the little girl's expression in a brief moment—and it had succeeded. Shelley wondered who the artist was. Surely not Vargen? Yet the boat was his. She sat down at the table and studied the three sketches. They were very good. She looked from them to the picture of the woman on the wall. If Vargen was the artist, had he done that one also? She wanted to know. She *had* to know.

Leaving everything where it was, she went out, up the steps, along the deck and up towards the cabin where Vargen was at the controls. He glanced round as she entered.

'Vargen,' she began, before she could have time to think about what she wanted to say and therefore make a mess of it, 'may I do some painting? I've found some canvases.'

'If you wish, of course.' He had looked away after that brief glance.

'Thank you. Er—I found some with sketches on. I

won't touch those, of course. Are they yours?'

He pressed a switch and the engine note died down slightly. He turned again, keeping one hand on the wheel. 'Why do you ask?' He was being completely un-approachable, almost dismissive, but she was learning fast now, and two could play at his game.

'Because they're good, and because I want to know.'

'Yes, they are.'

'And the picture of the woman on the saloon wall? Did you do that?'

His face tightened. It wasn't her imagination; it was like shutters coming down. 'Yes.'

She waited for him to say more, but he had finished. He had turned away, and the engine throbbed again into full life. The question trembled on her lips—who is she?—but she couldn't say the words. Silently she walked out and down, and away again, back to the saloon.

He had lied. He must have loved the woman as well, to paint her thus. Shelley found she didn't want to look at the picture any more. Instead she selected the watercolours and brushes, took a stack of thick car-tridge paper and set it on the table. The child's picture fascinated her. It was a challenge. If she could capture that on paper, then paint it, it would be interesting to see what she could accomplish. Shelley selected a soft black pencil from the box of them and began her task.

So engrossed was she that she was unaware of time passing, unaware even of the slowing of the yacht's en-gines and the stillness that followed. She had filled in the background with soft blue wash. She had found the sketch easy to copy, and more, had been able to use her imagination to supply the child's colouring. Deftly now she mixed skin tones until satisfied that she had the right tint, and began painting the little girl's face, so totally absorbed in her task that when Vargen's voice came from behind her she nearly knocked the paints over.

'Oh, you startled me!' she gasped. In a strange way she had almost forgotten where she was.

He stood looking down at what she was doing, his face expressionless. 'Do you want to eat now?' she asked, because she could hardly ask him what he thought of her efforts.

'Yes. But I will prepare the meal. Tonight we anchor here.' She looked up, turned, saw out of the window that they were moored in a bay, and only a dozen yards away lush palm trees curved gracefully towards the sea from a rocky beach. It could have been any island anywhere, it could be uninhabited, it could be the other side of Avala for all she knew—or at the end of the world.

'I didn't know we'd stopped,' she said, feeling foolish. She needed to get her balance back. She had been unaware of time passing, unaware of everything save what she was doing, and it was like coming back from another place to here—where the memories came back with that realisation. The memories of the raw, unleashed emotions that she had experienced. She turned back to her work, slowly, moving slowly, because she wasn't ready yet for it to happen again, and she knew it would, if not now, later, because the tension was raw and brittle, she could feel it building up now that Vargen stood in the room, and she wondered if he were angry again.

'Why did you copy that sketch?' he asked, and she looked up at him, because it was difficult to tell from his voice whether he was angry or just curious.

'I liked it. Besides, there's not much else to paint at sea,' she answered calmly. 'Do you mind me copying it?'

'No. I will go and prepare something to eat.' And he walked out. And thank you very much, Shelley said silently. You sure are a bundle of laughs! Damn you, damn the boat, damn everything! She glared at her half finished painting. She had suddenly lost interest in it—at least for now. She left it and went out to the galley to see Vargen searching through the refrigerator.

'Do let me get the meal,' she said. 'You've been steering the boat all afternoon, and I need to do something to pass the time.' She hoped the irony of that wasn't lost on him.

'As you wish. Thank you. I'll go and have a shower. It will be dark in a few minutes—the light switches are here.' He indicated them at the side of the door, and went out. He had put some bottles on the working surface and two glasses. There was a bottle of vodka, a white wine, and one of tonic. Shelley poured herself a good measure of vodka and topped it up with tonic, raised the glass, said 'Cheers,' and drank it. It made her feel quite better, so she poured another, drank that, and immediately wished she hadn't. The galley spun round alarmingly and she held on to the sink for a few seconds until it settled. 'Phew!' she gasped. Her head was very light and she wondered if she would float to the ceiling if she let go of the sink. She didn't want to find out. Very carefully she sat down on a stool and waited, and counted to ten. 'Wow!' It seemed a most amazing word, so she said it again, and began to giggle at the sound of it. She squinted at the bottle and wondered why it should have had that effect on her. She had drunk vodka before, and nothing like this had ever happened. Very, very slowly she stood up, to go and investigate this peculiar phenomenon, picked up the bottle, and found to her horror that she couldn't read the label.

For a moment she felt a wave of panic engulf her— and then realised that the label was in Russian, which made sense, and also seemed extremely funny. She began to laugh, and she was feeling much better now, so she poured herself another tiny drop—only unfortunately her hand wasn't very steady, as she found to her dismay, and the glass was nearly half full before she realised. She put the bottle down, spilling some, and gazed at the glass in giggly amazement. 'Did I do *that*?' she mused aloud, and hiccuped. She must pour it back into the bottle before *he* found out. Focussing very carefully on the bottle, she lifted the glass and held it at the rim and began to pour. 'Whoops-a-daisy!' It gushed down the outside.

Shelley put the glass down, then picked it up again. That hadn't worked. Oh dear. What now? Of course! The brilliance of her idea hit her. Pour some into his glass and tell him she'd made him a drink! How simple. She did so, then thoughtfully adding more tonic to what was left in her own, sipped it, to see if Russian vodka—now that she knew it was the genuine article— tasted any different from the English variety. It didn't, not really, only she had finished it before she remembered, dimly, that vodka isn't supposed to have any taste anyway, and it seemed a wasted experiment, except for one thing. She now felt gloriously happy.

The rapidly darkening room was full of shadows, and it was a haven of peace and tranquillity, hazily beautiful, and she wasn't sure if she wanted the lights on anyway, even if she could remember where the switches were, which she couldn't, so she found her way to the table, held on and lowered herself on to a seat very gently. She began to sing, humming softly and happily to herself, not bothering with the words, just the tunes, all the old favourite pop tunes she could remember.

It was quite a shock when sudden light dazzled her eyes and she looked up to see Vargen standing in the doorway. She blinked and covered her eyes with her hand. 'Wheee!' she gasped. 'Tha's bright!' she gave him a warm smile. He was blurred but very attractive-looking. 'I poured you a drink!' she announced.

He walked in, looked at the bottle, the pool surrounding it, then at her. 'How much have you drunk?' he asked, his voice very calm, very level.

Shelley raised her eyebrows. 'How much have you drunk?' she mimicked, in a prissy voice. 'Why? Is it rationed?'

Vargen picked up the bottle, and it seemed to her that he went slightly pale, although she couldn't be sure, because she wasn't seeing him very clearly anyway, what with the room waving—the sea must be very rough, she thought—and him sort of wobbling a bit when he moved.

'I do wish you'd stand still,' she murmured, not complaining, just passing a remark. She heard him answer, but she didn't understand the words, but they were forcefully said, and he was very angry, that much she knew, only now it didn't bother her. She found it quite funny, and began to laugh helplessly until the tears ran down her cheeks, and she closed her eyes and couldn't stop laughing, until——

Crack! her head was jerked sideways as Vargen slapped her face hard, and she gasped with pain and shock, and stared at him, her mouth falling open.

'Oh!' She started to stand, to try and hit him back, but he pushed her down roughly, grabbed her hair, held it, and forced a cup to her mouth.

'Drink that,' he ordered.

She fought, she tried to turn her head away, she struggled, but she was helpless, the grip on her hair too painful to resist. She smelt something sweet and vile, and Vargen said again: 'Drink that, or I will force it down you!' Shelley thought she would die, and cried, and tried to protest, but he moved behind her and held her head back, saying: 'Drink it—now!' and too frightened at his power and anger to do otherwise, she obeyed.

She barely made it to the sink in time. Half a minute later, sobered, strangely empty, and feeling that death was imminent, she felt herself being lifted and carried and laid down on a soft bed.

Then damp cloths were on her face, and she was being bathed and cooled in sweet-scented water. She kept her eyes tightly shut because she didn't want to see him or look at him because he was a monster who had struck her and hurt and tried to kill her, and she was too weak to fight. The nightmare faded as she felt him drying her face, her neck, her arms, but he wasn't violent now, he was being gentle. Her head spun round, but it was a different kind of whirling from before. Now it was a floating away, almost pleasant dizziness. She managed to open her eyes, and he was sitting on the bed, and she was lying on it, and he was looking at her.

She let out her breath in a long shuddering sigh, and he said: 'You'll be all right now.'

Tears filled her eyes. 'You hurt me,' she whispered.

'I had to strike you—I am sorry. You could have died.' Her head was clearing rapidly, and at those last words, some glimmer of realisation that he spoke the truth came to her. Wordless, she looked at him.

'What you were drinking was over a hundred proof —exceptionally strong vodka—did you not realise?

And you had taken nearly a third of a bottle. I made you sick, otherwise you would certainly have been very ill.' He put his hand on her forehead. 'Now you must eat.'

'No.' She shook her head feebly. 'I couldn't!'

'You will. Dry biscuits, and some fruit juice, that is all.' He went out quietly and Shelley was left to her thoughts. She didn't want to be alone, and she didn't want to be with him. She didn't know what she did want, only that there was an aching emptiness inside her that filled her very being, and she knew how he must despise her because of what she had done, and that was part of the aching and the loneliness. It mingled with her weakness so that the tears ran freely as if to wash away the hurt, but they didn't. Shelley turned on her side and held the pillow and sobbed.

The cabin was in darkness, sufficient light coming in from the one in the narrow passageway, and she was grateful that Vargen couldn't see her face when he returned, nor she his, only the vague blur of him.

'Sit up,' he said, and helped her. 'Please try and eat.' He carried a tray and put it on the floor, and gave her a plate with small round biscuits on. Shelley began to eat. They were dry, and quite sweet, and she ate several, then he handed her a glass of orange juice which she sipped alternately with the hard, sweet biscuits. After four she had had enough.

'No more,' she said. 'I couldn't.'

'Those will do. How do you feel now?'

How could she tell him? Or anybody for that matter? 'Better, thank you. I'm sorry I was so much trouble —I only thought of having a drink to——' she couldn't say that either, so she added: 'While I was preparing the meal.'

'I should have told you. You were not to know.' At

least he wasn't angry any more, or didn't seem to be. Her face ached with crying, and she was beginning to feel cold, and she still felt dizzy when she had sat up. She shivered, and he noticed.

'Are you cold?'

'Yes.' He felt her forehead again, and his hand was cool, and she felt as if her head was burning. She wanted him to leave his hand there, and made a small wordless sound of pain.

'It is better for you to go to bed and sleep.'

'I want a shower first. I'll feel better. Then I'll go.'

'Be careful, then. Try to stand.' She swung her legs over the side of the bed and stood up. He caught her as she swayed and for a moment she clung to him help-lessly.

'My head——' she muttered. 'It's——'

'Don't talk. Come, let me help you.' She felt like a child, walking slowly across the cabin—only a few steps—to her shower cubicle, and even that was an effort.

'This is so silly,' she murmured.

'Hush, do not talk. Easy now.' With infinite patience Vargen took her into the small cabin and turned on the shower. 'It is better to be warm. Not hot, or cold—just warm.' The water gushed out, splashing on the tiles, and she stood looking helplessly at it, wondering how she would manage. How could she hate him now? This hard, ruthless man was being anything but that. She had caused him infinite trouble in the last half hour, and he had every right to be contemptuous—but he wasn't being. He was totally impersonal, yet caring, like a nurse with a helpless patient, and Shelley knew, with the part of her brain that was functioning nor-mally, that she was helpless, and as yet there was noth-ing she could do about it. She still felt absurdly lightheaded and dizzy, but she was fighting for control.

'Thank you, I'll manage now.' She reached out to feel the water, and it was warm, just right. She steadied herself on the wall and looked at him. 'It's all right,' she said.

'I'll wait outside, in your bedroom. Just there.' He pointed.

'Yes. I'll not be a minute.'

'Don't lock the door,' he said.

'No, I won't.' She waited until he had gone out, leaving the door ajar, and remembered the last time she had been in a shower at the penthouse apartment, and left the door open deliberately. How different now! How could she have done that? She shivered, realising how Vargen must have remembered it too, on hearing her father's words.... She closed her eyes, sick at the memories, and the thoughts, then carefully, slowly, she peeled off her top, then the shorts, and stepped under the shower. There was a small shelf in the wall for the soap, and she found that if she held on to that, it steadied her. With her other hand she soaped herself, cleansing away the care of the day, the dust, the perspiration, feeling her skin tingle with cleanliness.

There would be no more defiance, no stupid gestures, no getting drunk, or nearly drowned. She would build up her shell, and be quiet and calm, self-possessed and safe. She moved, letting the water caress her face, her mouth, her closed eyes, and she began to feel so much better that she wanted to tell Vargen so. To let him know she was all right and independent. She turned the water off and it trickled into nothingness, a drip, drip, from the spray, then nothing. She reached for the towel on the door, but everything whirled round, stars filled her head, and she gasped with shock, 'Oh!' She grabbed the towel and leaned against the wall to recover her balance, and he shouted:

'Shelley? What is it?'

Hastily she wrapped the towel round her. 'Nothing. Just dizziness——'

He opened the door and came in to see her leaning against the cool tiles. She tried to smile reassuringly. 'I'm all right, honestly——' she began, then he caught her and held her, and led her into the cabin where she stood waiting obediently to be told what to do because it was easier not to have to think, because her head was spinning round.

He began to dry her with the other towel, while she stood there. He rubbed her soaking wet hair very carefully, but it hurt, and she put up her hands to stop him, to do it herself, and her covering towel slid gracefully to the floor and she stood there naked, and she began to shiver with the sudden cold.

'I'm sorry,' she began, and as she tried to bend down to pick it up, so did he, and their heads collided, and she would have fallen, but he caught her and the towel at the same moment, steadied her with his right hand while he began trying to wrap the towel round her with his left, and then suddenly it was different. Something changed, and they were both aware of it. His hand accidently touched her breast, and she felt that surge of sudden excitement fill her and knew, as surely as if he had said, that he was aroused. The simmering undercurrent of tension, never far away, never really dormant even in their more civilised moments, filled the room with an electrifying intensity so that her heart pounded, and she was skin-tinglingly aware of him as a dark, hard virile man.

Softly she half turned, helplessly caught up in the

wave of overwhelming pulsating awareness of this moment, where each breath, each simple touch, was a caress. The air sparkled and shimmered with the explosive power that needed only a spark to set it off.

It was as if everything began to happen in slow motion, so that each small moment took an age, and was as profound and deep as lovemaking. It was as though sparks of fire flashed at every slight movement, and Vargen's hand, the hand putting the towel round her, seemed to take an age to do it. She put her hand to her head and said, and the words seemed to echo from far away: 'I'll do that—my head hurts when you touch me,' and he said:

'I'm sorry, of course——' It was like a script that had been written for them, they mouthing words that were meaningless, because no words could possibly have the meaning of what was actually happening, because in some situations, no words can convey the truth, the inner meaning. Vargen put his hand to her face, with what seemed infinite slowness so that it was an eternity before he reached it, and said:

'Does it hurt there?' It was where he had struck her aeons ago, in another world, and she said:

'A little,' because although it didn't, that was what he wanted her to say, because the hidden language was all that mattered, not the words themselves. He murmured:

'Forgive me,' and stroked her cheek, and touched the tears that hadn't yet dried, then smoothed under her eye and then her eyebrow, as if he was discovering something new and very wonderful. Shelley made a little sound, a tiny murmur, and he put his other hand to her other cheek and held that too, very softly, very gently. The towel slid to the floor because he wasn't holding it any more, but she didn't remember that happening, and it didn't seem as if he noticed, or even if it mattered. He touched her hair, and ran his fingers through it very carefully so as not to hurt her head, then he bent and touched her cheek with his mouth, and moved his lips above it in a touch of fire so that it was warm, and said:

'Does that make it hurt less?' But the words were meaningless because it wasn't really what he was saying, or what she was replying that mattered at all, it was what was not being said that counted. From her hair he let his fingers slide slowly, gently downwards, leaving a trail of fire at his touch, that blazed and warmed her very being, tingling all through her, every inch of her. She stood there, no longer dizzy in the way she had been, but in a very different way, an entirely new way altogether that when he asked where she hurt, and she knew what she had to tell him, and did so, made her feel as if she might float away. She knew it was madness, but it was too late to do anything about it now, it was much too late. It had been too late the moment she married him, because she had known then what would happen, but she hadn't known when. And it was now.

His lips came down on hers, warm and sensual, and she put her hands round him, to hold him to her, because in that kiss was the question she was now answering, had already answered in everything but words, which were no longer necessary. She wasn't aware of them moving, because his kiss took her breath away, so deep and sensual was it, like the time before, in his apartment, when it had been everything—only now she knew it hadn't, because this was more, far more, and this would not end as that had, this would go on, and on. She felt the hard bed beneath her, and was aware of having been lifted and placed there, and she lifted up her arms to him, to pull him down to her, to hold him as she had never held anyone before. Her heart pounded so fast that she thought she would die, and then he was holding her as if he would never let her go, and Shelley knew, at last, with the last vestiges of her conscious mind, she knew the meaning of ecstasy.

There was only darkness, and movement, and two bodies that became as one, in the stillness and silence, with only the waves gently lapping against the boat, but unnoticed, and outside, in the cool evening air, the stars emerged into the black velvet of the sky, and a high clear moon shone down upon the still, dark sea. A breeze rustled the dry leaves of the palm trees on the island, and the yacht lay in the water, with one small light shining out into the darkness, and that was all. The hours blended, and darkness gave way to morning. The small light grew dimmer as the sun rose, and there was silence, and a great stillness, as they slept, at last, near dawn.

CHAPTER NINE

SHELLEY opened her eyes and looked at the sleeping man beside her, and felt a great surge of joy and love for him. How wrong she had been about him, how very wrong! She felt a warm contentment as she basked in the memory of his lovemaking, her body vibrantly alive and aware of him so that she reached out gently to touch him, to make sure he was real.

Vargen lay on his side, facing her, and as she touched his face gently with her cool hand he opened his eyes.

Then it changed. Suddenly it changed. She saw the look in his eyes—she had seen that look before—and she made a small, wordless murmur, and took her hand away as if it burned. Vargen muttered: 'Oh, *God*!' and she seemed to be hearing in his voice what she had just seen in his eyes, what he couldn't disguise, because in that first second of waking there is no time for pretence, and she had seen the contempt and loathing that had so shattered her after the kiss in his apartment when he had turned away from her.

She turned away from him now, and got out of bed and pulled on her wrap, then stumbled on leaden feet on to the deck. There she gripped the rail and stood looking out to the island, but she saw nothing of it, only his eyes, and face, and heard again the words: 'Oh, *God*!' as if he had, at the moment of waking, remembered what had happened, and despised her—and himself—for it.

She fought to control her breathing. Her heart was pounding fast, and hurt her, as the realisation washed over her. She had been still drunk, and had tempted him, and because he was a man who needed women, and used them, he had used her. The memories flooded back and she put her knuckles to her mouth to stop a cry escaping. He had used her—because she had been there. Not because he loved her, but simply because the temptation had been too great to resist. And who could blame him? Especially after what her father must have told him. Vargen would have had to be made of stone to have resisted what she had apparently been offering. She looked down at the water, feeling revulsion, feeling almost sick. After her behaviour with the bikini that previous afternoon he must have thought—what must he have thought? It was obvious. He must have thought—she's asking for it. He had been so gentle, so caring, after her brief madness with the vodka. But he must have been coldbloodedly planning—and she had made it easy for him, so very easy. Now, thinking clearly at last, she saw how every moment, which had been so wonderful for her, had just been leading up to the thing he wanted. To get her into bed.

She looked up at the sky, and, anguished, shook her head from side to side. 'Oh, no—no!' she muttered as if by saying the words, it could all be made not to have happened. But it had happened. But it had. And she, at last allowing her love to overwhelm her, had responded with joyous abandon to Vargen's skilful lovemaking. She closed her eyes. And he, thinking that no doubt she was as experienced as he himself was, had played his part well, had taken her, as casually as any of his other women—his mistresses—because that was all it was to him, a game, a physical need to be assuaged.

She didn't want him to come up on deck. She prayed that he wouldn't. Did his other women see that contempt? Perhaps so, but they wouldn't care, because it was a game to them as well. They would be sophisticated and as hard as he was, and they would know his marriage was a farce without being told, because they would know him as he really was.

It would be better if I were like that, she thought. He couldn't hurt me then. But he had hurt her, so deeply that it was painful to think about it. He wouldn't know that he was the first man to make love to her, and if she told him he wouldn't believe it, and she wasn't going to tell him. Let him think what he already did. And let me learn to be tough, Shelley said silently. And let it not matter what has happened. But her life would never be the same again, no matter what.

How should she behave now? She had to meet him some time. They would have to speak. How did a sophisticated woman behave? 'Darling, that was wonderful, we must do it again some time,' followed by a seductive laugh? Or casually, 'What would you like for breakfast?' As though nothing had happened out of the ordinary? She managed a small wry smile at that. If only that were possible!

Then she took a deep breath. Why not? She was learning fast. If she didn't let him see the real her, she would be safe. Now, before she had time to think about it too much, and falter. Now was the time. He need never know she had seen what she had seen in his eyes. She went back, down the steps into her cabin, took a deep breath and said:

'What would you like for breakfast?'

Vargen opened his eyes. 'Anything, thanks.' He was watching her, cool, hard, assessing. She smiled.

'Right,' and she swept out.

He came into the galley a few minutes later, fastening his shorts. Shelley had poured out two glasses of orange juice and was toasting sliced bread under the grill. 'I think the bread's better toasted,' she said. 'It's a bit stale.'

He sat down and she handed him the orange juice. 'If we're staying here today I'll do some painting on the island,' she said.

'We can do, of course.'

'Then that's what I'll do.' She made herself look at him just as though he was a breakfast companion, no more. 'And what will you do?' she asked.

He shrugged. 'I have first to make a few calls on the radio,' he answered. The hard eyes looked back at her. Did he seem puzzled? She couldn't be sure. She hoped so.

'Oh. Business, I suppose?'

'Yes.'

The toast was ready. She snatched it from under the grill and buttered it, put the apricot conserve on the table, then sat down herself.

They ate in silence, and Shelley ate quickly, wanting to be away. Anywhere, just as long as it was away from him. In fact, she was getting an idea that seemed very sensible. 'Could I take some food and drink with me?' she asked, 'then I can stay a while.'

'Of course.' Their eyes met across the table.

'Is the island uninhabited?'

'Yes. It is very small, as you will see for yourself.'

'Any animals or creepy-crawlies I should watch out for?'

He smiled. 'There are always insects, of course. Take some repellent spray with you.'

'Hmm. Only trouble is, how do I get it all ashore?'

'No problem. A large plastic container is all you need. You can pack your paints, food, blanket to sit on

—anything you like, in fact, then you push it ashore, or if you prefer, I will do it for you.'

'That's kind of you, but I think I'll manage. If you'll find me the plastic container I'll get everything I want packed in it.'

Vargen went over to one of the cupboards and fetched what looked like a huge laundry bag. The only difference was that the plastic was much thicker, and had a strong plastic zip top and a towing handle. He put it on the floor.

'Thanks. Can I take a towel or something to sit on?'

'Take anything you wish.'

She collected both plates and glasses and took them to the sink, and began to rinse them. She heard him go out, but didn't look round. The first—the worst—hurdle seemed to have been jumped. And she intended to stay out all day.

She filled a thermos jug with water, added ice, and put it on the table. Then she found some biscuits, an orange, an avocado pear, and added them. She went to the saloon for paper and paints and a small board, and when she got back to the galley Vargen was waiting with an aerosol spray.

'Give me your painting things,' he said. 'They can be wrapped together.' She handed them to him.

'I'll go and get dressed,' she told him, 'then I'll set off.'

She put on a clean T-shirt and shorts, found some flat sandals, and went back into the galley. The bag was packed for her. 'I've put in a large towel as well,' he said. 'Take care when you unwrap everything.'

'I will.' She pushed the sandals in and zipped it up. 'I'll see you later, then.'

'Yes.' He followed her up on the deck, carrying the

bag which he had taken from her, and handed it to her when she was nearly down the ladder. Shelley began to wonder if she was dreaming. The situation had a bizarre quality to it, quite unreal, so calm, so different from what had gone on before. She set off swimming, without once looking back, and the water was real enough. She reached the beach, opened the bag and put her sandals on. No more shells in feet! As she set off walking along the thick crunchy sand, she looked back. Vargen stood on deck, watching her. She waved and turned away, and when she looked round again he had vanished.

She walked until the yacht was just out of sight, found a cool spot beneath a large stunted palm, with rocks all around her, spread the towel out and sat down, careful to keep in the shade. Her shorts and top were already dry after her tiring swim, and she lay back, intending to have a rest for a few minutes, and to think.

When she awoke it was noon, the sun was high in the sky, and she was starving. She looked at her watch in disbelief. She had slept soundly for over three hours. She stretched and yawned, feeling much better for the sleep, peeled the avocado and ate it, then drank some water and had a couple of biscuits.

Then she set up her makeshift easel—the board—on her knee, and began to sketch her surroundings. Time passed at a special leisurely pace all its own. The air was sweet with a kind of honeysuckle smell that was almost soporific, and birds twittered in the trees above, and an occasional gull swooped close to see if there was anything interesting to see. One landed, and she drew that, and was pleased with the result. The place was certainly having its effect on her. It was superbly peaceful, the sea was calm and still, the tiny wavelets shushing into the sand and vanishing, the sun sparkling on the distant waves, edging them with molten gold. It was too nice to move, but Shelley wanted to explore the island, if only to find the flowers whose scent so fascinated her. It seemed pleasant to have to make a decision. To move or not to move, and no urgency either way. She thought about it for a while, had another drink of the still, cool water, then decided to explore now, come back and paint later.

She set off, leaving her things on the towel, and made her way through twisted palms and shrubs, now in shadow, now in sunlight, until she reached some large rocks surrounding a pool. Icy fresh water bubbled out of a rock and she stared at it in amazement and delight. The water was crystal clear, and she sat on a smooth rock and cooled her feet in it. The sun was on her body, and she tilted her head back and closed her eyes, enjoying the warm caress of the sun's rays. It was like an oasis in a desert here, and she decided she would have to paint it. There was shade nearby, and a flat stone to sit on. Once decided, she went back, collected her things and returned with them. She spread out the towel in the shade for later, sat on the flat stone, and began drawing the rock pool. Behind it the ground rose in a sandy rock-strewn mound, covered in more trees, and after painting for a while she climbed that and looked down at the island. She caught a glimpse of the yacht in the distance, through the palms, but she couldn't see Vargen. Sliding down the hillock again, she had a quick wash in the pool and went back to her stone. She felt tired, it was so hot, and lay down on the blanket and dozed for a while, after taking the precaution of spraying insect repellent over her.

When she woke up it was nearly five. She ate the orange and the last few biscuits, drank more water, leaving enough for one more drink, and picked up the painting of the rock pool, which was progressing nicely. She hadn't found the flowers, but she had found this place, and she knew she would remember her day here for ever. That, at least, she would want to remember. Some things were best forgotten, and would be, one day.

She went to the pool to get fresh water for her paints, and, leaning over, saw her face reflected in the water. Her eyes looked large and dark, and she smiled at her reflection, then grimaced. Soon she must go back. It would be dark within an hour and she had done enough stupid things already; she wasn't going to add getting lost to the list. She decided to paint for another twenty minutes, then pack up. She could finish the painting from memory afterwards.

She sat down, and became so engrossed that she forgot the time, and when she looked at her watch, it was too late. There was no twilight there; one minute there was light, the next it was dark. The air had gone cooler as well. Hastily Shelley began putting everything in the bag, leaving the painting till last so that it would be dry. She could see the sun over the horizon, spreading glorious reds and golds in a final blaze of colour, and her heart ached to see it. It was impossible to look away, to miss the rapid sinking down of the now, red sun as it appeared to sink into the sea itself, to be swallowed up.

'Shelley!' she heard the distant cry, and felt her skin prickle in resentment. Let him shout! She knelt and found her sandals; the last vestiges of light were disappearing rapidly and it was surprising how everything changed in just a few minutes. The dark shadows of the trees were larger, not as pleasant, and everything was dark and still. She turned to see the pool for the last time, and all she saw were dark rough shapes, of the rocks.

She heard his voice, nearer now, and answered. 'I'm here. I'm just coming!' and heard his footsteps crunching, coming nearer, and she picked up the bag. Then he was there, a dark blur, and she said: 'I know it's dark, but I was painting. I'm ready.'

'I thought you might be lost. I didn't know you were going to be away all this time,' he said.

'I could hardly get lost on an island this size,' she answered. 'And I didn't know I was supposed to get back at a given time.' She was very calm. She had had all day away from him, and it had been the best thing possible, but he didn't know that, of course, and if he got angry, she would laugh.

He came nearer. 'Let me take the bag,' he said. She handed it to him, and he turned and set off walking. As she followed, she remembered the painting which she had left out to dry.

'Oh, wait,' she called. 'I've left something.' She turned back, but could see nothing. 'Oh, damn,' she muttered. She heard him put down the bag.

'What is it?' he asked. Not impatient, not yet. Not amused either.

'The painting I was doing. I put it to dry on a rock——' She knelt, and began feeling round her in the dark. Now where on earth was it? There was the pool—or at least the shadows of the rocks, and she'd left it *there*—or had she?

She heard him make an impatient exclamation, and felt her temper rise. 'You go on,' she said. 'I'll follow.'

'Don't be silly.' He was by her now, and he crouched down, and she glared at him, only he couldn't see it in the dark.

'It was here, I'm sure it was,' she said. 'I was painting the pool, and that's *there*, and I was sitting on a flat stone here—only I can't find it——'

'*Chort!*' he said.

She didn't know what it meant, but it certainly wasn't a compliment. 'Listen,' she answered, keeping her voice quite calm. 'I am going to find it. What's your rush, anyway? I mean, do we have to be back for dinner *now?*'

'Shall I go and get a torch?' he enquired with heavy irony.

'Oh, I know it's not important to you,' she retorted. 'But I've spent all afternoon doing it, and it's important to *me*.'

He stood up, towering over her, making her feel very small. 'There is no need for you to be so angry,' he said. 'We will find it, if that is what you wish.'

'It is what I wish,' she said, and turned away. 'Or I wouldn't be looking.' Then she found it, and picked it up. 'I'll put it in the bag, then we'll go.' She walked over to the trees where he had left the bag, rolled the thick paper carefully up and placed it inside. He was behind her now and bent to pick up the bag, but she had been bending too, and straightened at the wrong moment, and collided with him so that he put out his hands to steady her, on her arms. The touch triggered off a reaction that was so instant and powerful that it was frightening. She jerked herself free by flinging her arms out, aside.

'*No!* Oh *no!*' she gasped breathlessly, and whirled away, and ran from him, into the thick trees. She heard him calling something, telling her to be careful, but she was heedless. She hadn't realised the effect his touch would have, the panic it brought to her so devastatingly. She was out of the trees now, and walking swiftly along the beach, ashamed at her childish reaction, but unable to have done anything else, and he caught her up, took her arm, and whirled her round to face him.

'I was trying to stop you from falling!' he snapped.

'Were you?' she flashed back. 'And I don't want you to *touch* me, d'you hear. Take your hand off my arm!' She tried to pull it away, but this time his grip was like steel, and she couldn't. She put her hand up to hit him, but he dropped the bag and caught her other arm before it could connect, then pulled her towards him and held her roughly.

'Don't you?' he grated. 'Or is it because you're frightened of *yourself*?'

'Well, I'm not frightened of you!' She breathed. 'I *loathe* you——' Her voice shook with rage. 'Can't you tell? I despise you!'

'Or do you despise yourself—for being human?'

'Well, you're certainly not!' she snapped back, and gathering all her strength together, made one almighty effort to be free, arching her body in a last frantic pull —and he released her so suddenly that she went sprawling on the sand. The fall winded her, knocked her breath out of her for an instant, then, as she recovered and he bent, she grabbed his arm and pulled hard, at the same moment trying to scramble to her feet. As he went down, caught off balance, he fell on her, and she instinctively lashed out with hands and feet, and felt them connect, and felt a surge of satisfaction as she heard his muffled gasp of pain. She pushed him away, rolled out from under, and scrabbled desperately in the sand to get herself away, out of his reach, before he recovered—and felt her ankle gripped as if in a vice, heard his voice: 'You little wildcat!' and kicked out at the sound.

Then—'Ouch—let me *go*!' she burst out frantically as he was on her again, and she pushed and struggled, but she was powerless—and they both knew it, Shelley lay there, helpless, on her back, and looked up at him crouching over her, keeping her down by the sheer weight of him, and by the steel bands that held her arms. She knew a surge of helpless, shivering excitement at what she saw in his face, so dark and shadowy—and angry. Not the anger of before, a different, harder anger, a pulsating, beating anger that she hadn't thought could exist. She lay still, because to move now would only increase that rage, and she was in no position to do anything about it except perhaps wait, her heart beating fast, for the inevitable punishment. Vargen looked angry enough to kill her—and he looked capable of anything—and she trembled and shivered, but she couldn't foresee the punishment he chose, and in that second when she did realise what it was, it was already too late.

He moved down, down, nearer, nearer, and she opened her mouth to cry out, but he silenced her with his own mouth, in a deep savage kiss that hurt her, that bruised her lips and left her so breathless that when the kiss was ended, she couldn't speak. 'Now,' he muttered, 'now—where is the fight?'

Shelley moaned and turned her head away, her mouth throbbing and sore. A shuddering gasp escaped her, and she felt the warm tears welling in her eyes, and she closed them. Then his hands were moving down her arms, to her hands, the weight of him disappeared, and he stood up, and as he did so he pulled her up with him to her feet and said: 'And if I had wanted to, I could have made love to you then.'

'Raped me,' she whispered, and put her hand to her aching mouth. 'You are despicable!'

'I am a man. Do you think I did not notice you flaunting yourself yesterday in that brief swimsuit—do you think I did not *know* you had done it deliberately?

Do you take me for a fool, Shelley? I am aware of what women can do——'

'Is that why you made love to me?' she snapped, filling the word love with contempt. 'I was a fool to let you near me after I'd had that vodka. Oh God, you had it all worked out, didn't you? The sympathy—the concern—all cleverly planned. I'll bet you even left the bottle out, knowing I wouldn't have a clue how strong it was—is that the only way you can get your women? To make them drunk first?' She laughed. 'Why, of course, it must be—you don't have anything else going for you, only your money—and I couldn't care less about *that*!'

She turned and marched away, praying that her legs wouldn't collapse under her, they were trembling so much. She walked into the water and swam the few yards to the boat, heard him behind her, but dared not look back. She had gone too far, and she knew it, and was frightened lest he see.

She reached the deck and ran down into the galley, and went to the sink for a drink of water; it was in darkness, but she didn't want the lights on. She didn't want Vargen to see her face. She heard him following, down the steps, quietly, barefoot, his footsteps almost sinister, like a stranger's and she didn't know what he would do. She knew, suddenly, why she had said what she had, and the pulse beat in her throat, and she turned away from the sink and watched him come into the galley, waited for him to put the light on, but he didn't, and he couldn't see her face, which was a relief, but it was unnerving as well. She wanted to get out of there, and went forward, but he stood in the doorway and looked down at her, and she saw the faint shadowy smile in the darkness, and said: 'Let me pass.'

'When you have explained the meaning of your remarks,' he said. He spoke very quietly, calmly. It might have been better had he shouted.

'They don't need explaining——'

'I think, yes, they do.'

'Well, I'm not going to.' She stood, arms akimbo, and faced him. 'And don't worry, I'm not going to drink anything like that again. Once is enough for me.'

'I imagined your reaction, did I? That was outrage, and shock—not desire, when you responded? Did I also imagine your reaction in my apartment? When you lay on the bed——'

He got no further because she hit him, to silence the dreadful, unbearable words. She heard his indrawn breath and stepped back instinctively, landing against the table as he moved forward and took her by the arms and pulled her towards him.

'No,' he said, and his voice was harsh. 'You do not hit me again——' and he bent his head and found her mouth with his own; he kissed her savagely, while she fought and struggled and knew that he was going to make love to her again, and knew that she wanted him with every inch of her being. And because she knew, and was ashamed of her own weakness and longing, she fought and struggled the more, but knowing a growing excitement within her, corresponding to his. Then the struggles became less intense as the magic touch of his lips, the deep hard intensity gathered into a single explosive point of contact, worked their power, and she abandoned herself to his arms, to the rough punishing caresses that changed and became subtly gentler, and in so being, more powerful.

His mouth was at her throat now, kissing the tell-tale pulse, as with his hands he eased the T-shirt upwards

and teased her body with his fingertips in a featherlight
touch that left her breathless with desire and wanting.
When he lifted her up, she made no protest at all. And
when he carried her into her cabin and closed the door,
and put her down at the side of the bed, she slid her
arms out of her T-shirt and flung it on the chair and
sat down. He sat beside her, looking at her, gazing at
the shadowy outline of her, and gently then he pushed
her down beside him, and found her mouth again, and
teased her slender body with skilful hands that knew
what they were doing, only too well, so that minutes
later, unable to bear the waiting, she caught his hands
and held them, and he said: 'Tell me what you want
me to do,' as he bent his head to her. She told him,
and he said: 'Say it again,' and she bit his ear, and
he laughed, softly, secretly, and said: 'Very well——'

Shelley gave a deep, shuddering sigh of impatience,
and it seemed that time stood still for the next few
moments—then the waiting was over. . . .

When she awoke the following morning she was alone.
She lay for several minutes surfacing through layers of
sleep, and remembering all that had passed, lay very
still, scarcely breathing, her whole body and mind
aflame with the memories. Once again she had betrayed
herself, and Vargen had made sure she knew it. How
very clever he was! Subtle, strong, cunning—how could
anyone stand a chance against that combination? And
there were two more days to go. . . .

She got up and showered, then, feeling extremely
hungry, went to the galley. There were no signs of
Vargen, although there was evidence that he had break-
fasted. Shelley made herself strong black coffee, some
toast, and sat down to eat it. She heard sounds from

above, footsteps, then his steps on the stairs, and a moment later he appeared at the door. Shelley took a deep breath, then looked up.

'Hello,' he said. There seemed to be amusement in those tawny eyes, and she felt her face muscles tighten helplessly, and forced herself to respond.

'Hello. You've eaten?'

'Yes, a while ago. Would you mind if we returned to Avala today?' She looked at him. Mind? She had been wondering how she could tell him that she didn't want to be on a boat with him any longer; that if she stayed, she would probably go mad. . . .

'Mind? I don't mind. Any particular reason?'

'Business. I had to call Bruno again this morning—something's cropped up.'

'When do we leave?'

'Any minute.'

Shelley stood up and carried her plates to the sink. 'I'll put these away.' When she looked round again, Vargen had gone. She washed the dishes, returned them to their places in the cupboard, and heard the deep throb of motors starting up. Goodbye, island, she thought, and goodbye, honeymoon.

At least on Avala there would be other people. There would be Uncle Victor, and Eileen, places and people to visit. Human contact, warmth—she needed that. She needed an antidote to Vargen, and back on Avala she would make sure she got it.

She felt the boat start to move, sliding away effortlessly from the unnamed island, and watched it recede, become smaller and smaller. Then she went to pack her clothes. An hour or so later she took a cool drink up to Vargen at the controls.

'What time will we be back?' she shouted above the roar of the engines.

'In about six hours. I am at full speed now.'

'Do you want food?'

'In a while. Avocado and cheese will do.' He swallowed his drink in one go and handed her the empty glass. 'Thank you.'

She left him. Six hours. That would make it mid-afternoon for their arrival, and home to their apartment. She would telephone Victor and arrange to see him. Then what? The next six months seemed to stretch in an eternity of time. It wouldn't pass quickly, it would be for ever....

She washed her underwear by hand and spread it out on deck to dry, cleaned the galley and stripped the beds ready for their arrival. She was restless and uneasy. To soothe herself, she set out her painting things on the deck, sat in the shade on the lounger, and continued her painting of the child. The therapy worked, and she gradually began to feel calmer. It would be all right—soon. Vargen would have his women; he had made love to her twice—but that would be all. He had used her, as he had used every other woman who ever crossed his path, but he felt only contempt or, worse, indifference, for her. Which was worse? She looked out to sea and thought about that for a few minutes. It was no use kidding herself, he was a very experienced and skilful man; he had used his skills to full effect, and she had responded. But not any more. She looked down at her painting again. Not any more. There would be no more lovemaking, ever.

One day she would find another lover, and she would forget Vargen Gilev. Forget him? she thought. I wonder if that's possible? The picture blurred slightly, and she blinked and took a deep breath. It was time to get his lunch. She put her board to one side and went down to the galley.

Afterwards she lay down on the lounger in the shade, and closed her eyes. A cool breeze from the sea, and the movement from the yacht, teased her hair, and she found herself drifting into a doze, in which she had bright colourful dreams of life with Vargen, of dinners, business meetings with Bruno, and smiles and laughter, and a good pretence at being a happily married couple, loving, warm. . . .

When she opened her eyes, feeling happy and loved, it was to see the shoreline approaching. It was Avala. The dreams were over. They were home—and now began the reality of their shabby deception, the reality of the next six interminable months of life with a man who wasn't really human, nor ever would be. Shelley stood up and went to the rail, watching the island gradually take shape and form, and she lifted her head proudly. This then was the beginning.

CHAPTER TEN

SHELLEY dined that evening with her uncle and Eileen at Eileen's apartment. Vargen had driven her there, gone in with her, kissed her lightly on the cheek, and apologised to them all for having to leave for an important business meeting. After promising to return for her at eleven he had left, and Shelley, smiling at her uncle, had been surprised to see that he clearly considered all was well. Such was the power of Vargen to deceive!

Eileen batted her eyelashes and grinned at Shelley. 'He's gorgeous,' she whispered. So she didn't know. Or if she did, she was, like Uncle Victor, prepared to go along with the pretence. And why not? thought Shelley. They've got more sense than me, perhaps. She laughed. 'Isn't he?'

Uncle Victor hugged her. 'Nice to have you to ourselves for an evening,' he said. 'Eileen's been preparing things ever since you phoned. We consider ourselves very honoured you've chosen us for company your first evening back.' He looked thoughtfully at the door Vargen had only minutes before walked through. 'Everything all right?' he asked very casually.

'Fine,' lied Shelley. 'Just fine.' She gazed round the airy apartment. 'This is a super place, Eileen. Do you do your writing here?'

'I do. But Victor's probably told you we've got designs on a villa the other side of the island. We'll show you soon. I think you'll like it—I love it. And there he can paint and I can write my best seller—I hope!—and you can visit us as often as you like.'

'I'd love to.' It reminded her of Vargen's talent for painting, and she told them of the canvases she had found, and her own attempts at painting the rock pool, and the conversation was led safely away from any potentially dangerous topics.

They ate dinner by the small verandah. Eileen was a superb cook who had gone to a great deal of trouble, and the meal passed in an enjoyable, leisurely way. Afterwards they sat and had coffees and liqueurs, and Shelley began to feel relaxed. She loved her uncle dearly, and Eileen was warm and bubblingly irresistible. Shelley knew why he loved her, and hoped they would be happy together. She had forgotten the time, and it was quite a surprise, when she heard the telephone ring, to look at the clock and see it was nearly eleven.

It was Vargen on the telephone. Victor called her into the hall and she took the receiver from him. 'Hello?'

'Shelley, I am so sorry, something rather urgent has come up, and I shall be longer than I thought. Would you like to wait there or shall I send a car for you?'

'How long will you be?'

'At least another hour.'

'You'd better send the car, I'm rather tired.'

'Very well.'

'Goodbye,' she said, and hung up. She didn't want to hear his excuses, if indeed he intended to make any. Did he think she was a fool? Bruno would hardly keep his newly married godson from his bride. There was a perfectly logical explanation for Vargen's call, but she didn't intend to think about it yet. She went back into the lounge, smiling brightly. 'Vargen's been detained,' she said. 'He's sending a car for me.'

'Oh, shame,' said Eileen, pulling a face. 'Still, that's business, honey. Never mind. Can I call you tomorrow? I'd love to have someone to go round the shops with—men don't understand, do they?'

Shelley laughed. 'I'd love that. I need a few things myself. We can make a day of it if you like, lunch out and browse round the dress shops.'

'It's a date. I'll call you about eleven, okay?'

'Fine.'

She began to collect her things together, stole, hand-bag, sandals that she kicked off before, then the bell rang, and it was Vargen's driver. She hugged both of them, thanked them for a lovely evening, and set off to make the lonely journey back to the hotel. She left them standing at the door of the apartment, and as she rode home, saw again their faces, the happiness, the sheer togetherness of the scene. She felt very lonely.

The penthouse apartment was softly lit, and someone had set out a bottle of wine and two glasses on the table. There was also a freshly made pot of coffee, cream and cup and saucer. Shelley poured herself a cup and sat down by the open window. This then was to be the pattern of her life. She sensed very strongly that Vargen had begun as he intended going on, and however subtle and polite the message, it was there. He would lead his life, and allow her to lead hers. She sat back and sipped the coffee, wondering which of his women he had gone to see. She wondered if he would stay out all night, knowing she wasn't waiting at Eileen's apartment for him. She wondered if he had given her a single thought all evening. And lastly, she wondered where he was at the moment. And she thought she would never know. But the following day, she found out.

*

She woke up from a deep troubled sleep at four o'clock in the morning and heard someone moving quietly about the lounge, but it was the sound of something falling that woke her. Shelley sat up, picked up her wrap and crept out to investigate. She was not wide awake enough to worry whether it was an intruder— but it wasn't, it was Vargen. He was fully dressed, standing by the window looking out, and he turned slowly as he heard her, and looked at her.

Shelley took a deep breath. Now was the moment. If she made a hash of it, let him see her true feelings, she was lost. She sensed that this was a very significant moment in her life, but she didn't know why. Only a deep primitive instinct for self-preservation, for keeping the shell intact, was working strongly. 'Hello,' she said. 'Want a coffee?'

'Please. I'm sorry if I woke you,' he said, and there was something odd about his manner. Something she couldn't place; a certain—hesitation, for want of a better word.

'I heard something fall, that's all, so I came out to see. Sit down, I'll get you a coffee.' She went into the kitchen and put the kettle on. Was he drunk? He didn't seem to be, but then she didn't know how he'd behave if he were. Had he come straight from one of his mistresses? She didn't know, she wasn't going to show herself up by asking, she was going to be perfectly calm, as if it didn't matter a damn what time he came back, if at all. Then she'd be safe, because he wouldn't know.

She made two cups and carried them in. He had taken off the dinner jacket and stood in his shirtsleeves; he looked exhausted, and there were deep lines of fatigue round his mouth, and his eyes were shadowed. 'There you are. I'll have one as well,' she said, and sat down. From the settee she looked up at him. 'It's a good job I *didn't* wait for you at Eileen's,' she remarked pleasantly, and smiled.

Vargen sat down, near, not too near. 'I would have telephoned again, of course,' he said. 'I wouldn't have left you there all this time.'

'No, of course not.' She bent and picked up her handbag from the floor where, presumably, it had fallen.

'I'm sorry, did I knock that over?'

'It doesn't matter,' she said. 'Nothing breakable.' She sipped the hot coffee slowly. For the first time ever, with him, she felt totally in control of herself, and possibly the situation. She had blanked out her emotions and felt completely neutral, as though he were a stranger. Her own half waking state helped. It was too early to think very clearly, or to feel very strongly, about anything. Vargen, too, looked—different. He looked as though he had been through something terrible. He looked drained, exhausted—almost ill. She hadn't thought she would ever feel pity for him, but she did.

'Are you all right?' she asked.

He rubbed his forehead. 'Yes.' Then he looked at her. 'Why do you ask?'

'You don't look very well. Was the business meeting exhausting?'

For a moment he looked as though he didn't know what she was talking about, then he nodded. 'A little. I have a headache, that's all.'

'Oh dear!' She put her cup down and stood up. 'You should have said. I'll get you two aspirins—stay where you are, I know where they're kept.' She walked steadily towards the kitchen, everything under control, yet her heart had begun to beat faster. She didn't know why, precisely, except that her own calmness surprised her, and she knew he was very aware of it, and that he was anything but calm.

'There you are,' she handed him the bottle. 'Have two with your coffee.' She looked at her watch. 'It's past four. You won't be up in the morning if you don't get to bed soon. What time do you want me to get up?'

'Any time you wish. I will eat at eight-thirty——'

'That will suit me fine. I'm going out with Eileen for the day. That's all right with you, of course?'

'Of course. Do you need any money?'

'I've enough for the present. When I do, I'll ask.' He seemed to be having difficulty opening the childproof lock on the bottle, and Shelley took it from him.

'Here, let me.' She shook two out on her palm and held her hand out to him. 'There you go.'

'Thank you.' He took them, put them in his mouth, swallowed coffee. He really didn't look well at all, and she had to firmly suppress the small feeling of satisfaction. She smiled gently, to hide it.

'I'll say goodnight then, Vargen.' She stood up and looked down at him. 'Are you sure you can manage?'

'I've got a headache, that's all. I'm not crippled,' he said harshly, and she raised her eyebrows at the vehemence of his tone, and bit her lip to stop the sudden laughter escaping.

'Dear me,' she said mildly. 'Perhaps it's more a hangover—still, I'm sure you know how to deal with *those*.' She looked pointedly at the still unopened bottle of wine on the table. 'Shall I put that away?'

He stood up, tall, so tall and powerful, and—angry. 'I'm not drunk,' he said. 'I've not been drinking.'

'I didn't say you *had*. I merely thought you *might* have.'

'And don't humour me!'

'I'm not,' she retorted. 'I'm trying to help, that's all.

However, it seems as though I'll help more by getting out of your way. Have you finished with your coffee cup? If you have, I'll take it. I'm going back to bed to the sleep I was enjoying when you came in—just do as you wish, I don't really care either way.' She bent to pick up the coffee cup, and he bent at the same moment, and it was knocked over as she tried to move out of the way of his hand, because however calm she might be, she didn't want him touching her. The coffee spread over the table, and she made a small exclamation and glared at him.

'Now look——' she began, and turned to get a cloth from the kitchen, then saw his face as he swayed, put his hands to his face, and she caught hold of his arm. 'Vargen!' She felt the hard muscle of his arm under her hand, felt the sheer animal strength of him, and she knew that so well, but now it seemed as if he was going to fall, and she was suddenly scared. 'Be careful,' she said. 'Sit down——'

'I'm all right. There's nothing wrong with me,' he grated, and he moved, moved away from her, as though he didn't want *her* to touch *him* either, and she felt a sudden surge of overwhelming anger, and fought it, clenched her hands tightly to control herself, and snapped:

'Isn't there? Well, bully for you. Excuse *me*, I'll get something to wipe that mess up,' and stalked past him.

She slapped the cloth down on the table, ignoring him completely. If he wanted to fall about all over the place, he was welcome to do so, she was going to bed. She wiped up the spilt coffee and saw him walk away, towards the three steps, and watched him with a strange kind of detachment as he went. He went up them, and paused, and Shelley bit her lip, followed him, and said: 'Wait.'

She flung the cloth into the kitchen and went back to where he waited, ashen-faced. 'Come on,' she said. 'To bed,' and she took his arm. In her bedroom she said: 'Lie down. You can have my bed,' and he sat down on the edge of it, very still, like a man in a dream. Shelley debated whether to telephone down for a doctor, and after a moment, as he lay back, said: 'Look, I'd better get someone——'

'No,' he said fiercely. 'I need no one.'

'You're ill. Don't you understand, Vargen?' She sat down beside him, careful not to touch him.

'There is nothing wrong—nothing,' he answered fiercely. 'I will not see a doctor. Do you understand?'

'All right,' she soothed. 'Let me sponge your face, though.'

She came in with a damp washcloth and, before using it, put her hand to his forehead. It was very hot, and beaded with perspiration. She smoothed the damp cloth gently over his face, and he closed his eyes, lying very still.

'Is that better?' she asked.

'Yes. Thank you.'

'Then lie still.' She took off his shoes, and he loosened the collar of his shirt, but even that seemed to exhaust him, and he lay back, eyes closed, his face almost grey in the shadowy light. Then, as she sat there, just watching, his breathing became deeper, and she knew he had fallen asleep. That was a relief. Whatever was wrong with him, and she had no idea what it was, sleep would surely do him good. Very quietly she stood up, went to the other side of the bed, and lay down. She intended to stay for a while, to make sure he was properly asleep, then go into his bed in the dressing room, but gradually she felt her eyes going heavy, and heavier. It was too much effort to move, and Vargen was sleeping soundly now, so she reached down for the sheet in a last conscious effort, put it over them both, and fell asleep.

She was woken up by the pressure of weight on her, and she opened her eyes to see that he had moved and, still deeply asleep, imprisoned her with his arm, which lay across her. His head was against her bare shoulder, and his face, touching her skin, was cooler, almost normal. Shelley lay very still, enjoying the closeness of him when he couldn't possibly know about it, and thought back to the strange incidents of only hours previously. She had been concerned that he had a fever, and his behaviour had certainly been very odd and disturbing—then she remembered her own calmness in the face of it, and felt pleased that she had successfully overcome the temptation to hurt him. Oh, Vargen, she thought. If only you knew—— She closed her eyes, knowing she would manage to cope, to hide her own true feelings, because he had proved that it could be done.

It grew lighter outside, and warmer, as the sun filled the room, and still Vargen slept as if exhausted, and Shelley was content to be there with him even though soon everything would be back to normal. She moved slightly to make her shoulder more comfortable, and he murmured something in his sleep that sounded like—— 'Love you,' and she went cold. Was that what he had said to a woman last night? Was he dreaming of her, remembering? And did he tell them he loved them because they wanted to hear it, even though he would never mean it? He would never say it to Shelley. He never had, not even when he had taken her and made love to her with an overwhelming passion and need. He had never said it, not once.

I love you, she thought, even though I know I

shouldn't, I can't help it. And for a moment she allowed herself the fantasy that he had said the words to her, and it was like a warm glow inside her—just for a few brief seconds.

Then he moved. She felt his head shift slightly, and he made a small sound, as though puzzled, and lifted his arm, as if wondering what it was doing lying across her. She turned her head and saw him open his eyes, and said quickly, without giving herself time to think about it: 'I'm sorry—but you weren't well, and I was only trying to help——'

He looked at her blankly for a moment. 'I can't remember anything,' he said softly. 'I only remember having a terrible headache——' He paused. 'Where was I?'

'In the lounge. I heard a sound about four o'clock, and went in, and you were there. I made you a cup of——'

She stopped, felt her whole body go suddenly cold as he slid his arm across her again, brushing against her breast. She couldn't breathe. Fighting for calm, she said: 'A cup of coffee, and I ——'

He was touching her face now, in puzzlement as if still half asleep and not understanding what she was saying. He was stroking her cheek gently with a fingertip as if it was something new that he hadn't seen before, and she wondered if he was delirious and said desperately: 'I gave you two aspirins—do you feel all right?'

'Can't think,' he murmured. 'It's very blurred—where am I?' He must be delirious.

'Surely you recognise your own bedroom,' she said, and stopped. Her heart was beginning to thud. His hand was at her neck, holding it gently.

'Mmm?' he said. 'Bedroom? This is——'

'M-my bedroom——' It was ridiculous. He couldn't know what he was doing. Of course he couldn't. 'Look, I'd better go and——'

Vargen slid one leg over her, and imprisoned her with it. 'I feel so heavy,' he said, and his words seemed to be getting slurred. She had a moment of panic as she thought that he was clearly ill again, and said:

'You're heavy, I mean your leg's heavy. Why don't you move it and I can get——'

Her words were lost as he slid nearer to her and touched her face again, then pulled her towards him and moved his head and looked down at her. Then he closed his eyes as if he didn't want to keep them open any longer—then kissed her.

Shelley struggled, briefly, then felt herself weaken. Vargen moved, and put his arms round her, holding her to him, and said: 'Don't let me go, help me, Shelley, don't let me go——'

'It's all right,' she answered, fighting for sanity, struggling to keep her head, to help him, to soothe him, even if it meant staying, because he was obviously in need of help, and she had only a moment or two to realise that if he was so ill he shouldn't be so strong—before it was too late to worry about anything at all.

CHAPTER ELEVEN

Nothing had changed. Had she really expected it ever would? Shelley sat back in the car taking her to Eileen's apartment, and there was a dryness in her throat. When Vargen had been ill, so briefly, she had sensed a softening in his manner, a gentleness she had not known before—but it hadn't lasted, and when she had told him at breakfast that she was going out with Eileen, he had looked at her, and for a moment she had seen what seemed to her to be anger in his eyes. 'Do you have to go today?' he had asked, and Shelley had answered:

'No—but I'm going. Why? Do you expect me to sit here every day awaiting *your* return?'

'Of course not.' His face was very hard. Nothing wrong with him now, she thought wryly. He's back on form. 'Couldn't she come here?'

Shelley had risen from the table. 'We can hardly shop here, can we?' she had retorted. 'I'm going to call her now.'

'Wait. Will you go in the car?'

'To meet her? It's not that far to walk——'

'I'd rather you did.'

It seemed pointless to argue. She had shrugged. 'All right.'

'And let Alfredo bring you back as well?'

'I'm not a child!' she had snapped, and she remembered now, as she sat in the car, being driven by Alfredo, his expression as she had said it.

'Nevertheless, I insist,' said Vargen, and she was puzzled and disturbed by his words.

'All right,' she said. But she had no intention of doing so. It was as though he wanted a check on her movements, and I'm damned if *he's* going to do that, she thought.

She moved the window aside between her and the driver. 'Alfredo,' she said, 'I'll be going to the shops with my friend, so I won't need you after you've dropped me.'

Alfredo, a middle-aged native of Avala, looked at her through the driving mirror. He was unfailingly courteous, and she liked him. 'Madame?' he said, looking worried. 'Mr Gilev has told me that I am to meet you when you have finished your shopping.'

Shelley smiled. 'I know. But it's not necessary. I don't know how long we'll be—and I'd hate you to waste your time just watching for me to call.'

'Mr Gilev says that I am to be at your disposal all today.'

'Does he? That's very kind of him, but perhaps he doesn't understand what we women are like when we wander round the shops.' She laughed, as if it was all a pleasant joke, but her heart hardened. Damn the man! Who the hell did he think he was? Her *father*? And she slid the window closed, effectively ending the conversation. They were nearing Eileen's apartment now. She felt stifled, like a prisoner. And very determined.

Alfredo came round to open her door, and she waved at Eileen who was standing on the balcony of her apartment.

'Madame,' he said unhappily, 'I don't like to disobey Mr Gilev——'

'I know you don't, Alfredo, and I admire your loyalty. But I can't be tied down——'

'Any time you wish. Any time at all,' he said anxiously.

She softened. 'All right, I'll call you when I need you. Thank you for bringing me.' She walked towards the door, which Eileen had left open. But she had no intention of calling him. There wasn't much Vargen could do about *that*.

She hugged Eileen, who said: 'Let's have a cold drink before we set out, shall we?'

'Hmm, I'd love one.' Shelley sat down on the settee in the large cool apartment, and looked round admiringly. Eileen's taste was simple, and the furniture was light and uncluttered, and she had many pictures on the white walls, and several large ferny plants. 'I do like this place,' she said.

'So do I. But you should see the villa!'

'I'd like to do that too. When?'

Eileen brought in two frosted glasses full of amber liquid, ice clinking gently on the surface. 'Two Avala specials,' she said. 'And I'll show the villa to you any time you want. Tomorrow?'

'You're on.' Shelley raised her glass. 'Cheers.' She sipped the icy drink. 'Mmm, gorgeous. Not too alcoholic, I hope?'

Eileen smiled. 'Not too much.'

'But what about your writing? Don't let me keep you from that!'

Eileen shrugged. 'I'm between books at the moment, and putting off the dread moment when I have to start another—believe me, I'm only too happy to see you. I must introduce you and Vargen to some of my friends here. There's quite a colony of writers and artists on Avala. Is he a social animal?'

Shelley pulled a little face. 'I don't really know—yet,' she confessed, with a smile to show that it didn't matter. One day soon, she knew she would tell Eileen all about Vargen, but not yet. Eileen might already know about the bizarre marriage. If she did, she didn't show it. She was warm and kind, and clearly the soul of tact. Shelley liked her very much.

'We'll see won't we?' Eileen grinned back. 'Now tell me, what kind of things are you after?' They launched into a discussion about clothes, and shortly afterwards set off to walk to the shops. And Shelley was not aware that she was being followed.

She left Eileen late in the afternoon. She had bought several dresses at the large store, where Rosa and Pelma had served them both, and been persuaded to leave the clothes to be delivered later that day. She left Eileen outside, arranged to meet the following day, and set off walking, with a delightful feeling of guilt at disobeying Vargen. She nearly laughed out loud at the thought, but restrained herself.

She stopped in a quiet side street to look in a jeweller's window at a dazzling display of rings and bracelets and gorgeous pendants, and a woman's voice said in her ear:

'Excuse me—are you Mrs Gilev?'

Shelley looked round to see a tall elegant blonde smiling warmly at her.

'Yes,' she answered, surprised.

'Can I talk to you for a moment?'

'What about?' Shelley didn't like her, but without reason. It was just an instinctive dislike.

'I'm a friend of your husband's, Mrs Gilev. My name's Helena.'

Shelley felt herself go cold. Helena? The Helena of the yacht? She certainly bore no resemblance to the portrait in the salon. She looked into amused green eyes and felt a pang of jealousy so strong that she could hardly conceal it.

She hurried slightly away. 'I don't think there's much to say,' she said coolly.

'Oh, but there is. There's a lot to say. Like—where he was last night, for instance.'

Shelley turned, very slowly. 'My *husband* was at a business meeting,' she said, her voice icy.

'Is that what he told you?' The woman called Helena smiled slightly. 'He was with me.'

Shelley looked her up and down. She gripped her bag tightly to stop herself from raking her nails down the other's mocking face. She had gone icily cold inside—and icily controlled.

'Really? Do you think it interests me? Do you think I even believe you?'

She turned away again and started walking. Helena followed, and caught her arm. Shelley whirled round and clawed the other's hand away. 'Don't *touch* me again!' she breathed. Helena stepped back slightly, alarm flaring in her eyes, followed immediately by anger. Her eyes sparkled, and she looked at the hand Shelley had scratched slightly.

'You'll regret that,' she said in low tones.

'Will I? How?'

'Because——' She stopped, smiled, and nodded, and Shelley, sensing someone behind her, turned, and was caught in a firm grip by a man.

'What the hell——?' she began, struggling, then she saw the large dark car that had glided silently up to the curb and waited, engine purring, and door wide open. Too late she screamed, and the scream was muffled as a man's hand clamped over her mouth and she was pushed violently into the car, where she sprawled on the back seat. The whole incident had taken only seconds—Shelley pulled herself up to see two men sitting in the front of the car, and Helena beside her. She scrambled across to open the other back door, and it was locked. She pushed violently, but the car was already speeding away from the quiet street, leaving two children, the only witnesses, standing there puzzled.

Shelley launched herself on Helena, who spat out invective, and fought back. A voice from the front of the car, a very familiar voice said:

'Don't struggle, Shelley. It won't do you any good.' Then the man beside the driver turned round—and it was her father.

Shattered, she sat back limply, and stared unbelievingly at him. 'Father!'

'Yes. And I'm taking you home, my dear. Did you really think I'd give up so easily?' he laughed.

'Home?'

'To England. Where else?'

They were speeding out of the town now, and Shelley looked desperately out of the back window. There were no cars in sight, no traffic at all. But she knew they were on their way to the airport.

'Why?' she asked. 'Why?' The woman Helena might not have been there. She was no longer important. She sat in her corner of the car and looked at Shelley with hate in her eyes, but Shelley was unaware of it. She was aware of her father's face—and his expression, which was of a quiet triumph, a catlike satisfaction that made her feel ill.

'Why, my dear? There'll be plenty of time to explain on the journey out of here. Then you'll understand why, well enough. Nobody defies me—I thought you might have learnt that over the years, but it seems not.'

'You'll never get on a plane—I'll scream the place down——'

'I have a hired plane waiting at the airport. A private plane, you understand?'

An icy fear filled her. She knew he spoke the truth. Now at last she knew why Vargen had wanted her to be driven by Alfredo. With his knowledge of the island, he must have been aware that her father was still there. And now it was too late. Why, oh, why hadn't he told her? She would never know, because she would never see him again.

She closed her eyes. Would he even care? He was officially married, the partnership was going ahead— Bruno need not even be told she was no longer on Avala. It would be easy enough for a clever man like Vargen to conceal her disappearance with the excuses of illness, or other engagements, or perhaps even a visit to England to sort out her affairs there.... And time would pass, and then it wouldn't matter.

She felt physically sick, but even so, her mind worked with thoughts of escape. Yet her chances were slim, she knew that. She mentally braced herself. Let it appear that she had given in, was too overwhelmed....

She kept her eyes closed, but her hand was on her bag, and she desperately tried to remember what was in it that might serve as a weapon. Keys? She had those to the penthouse apartment, and a wallet, and a cologne spray, and a comb. And that was all.

'Who's she?' she said dully, as if it were an effort to think.

'She? You mean Helena? Oh, she knows Vargen, my dear. I made it my business to find people who knew him in those two days you were away. I've been very busy, in fact.' He laughed. Shelley opened her eyes and looked at the sleek, beautiful woman near her. She thought what she would like to do to her if she got the chance, and it made her feel fractionally better.

Helena laughed as well, and smiled at her father, and Shelley sank back into her seat as though it was too much for her to take, as it nearly was, but she was a fighter, and she wasn't going to go without leaving Helena something to remember her by. She fumbled in her bag for her handkerchief, dabbed her eyes with it, and concealed the comb in the palm of her hand.

They were nearing the airport now. She could see it, the long empty runway, the distant buildings—and, much nearer, one solitary plane parked at the farthest edge of the field. A small orange truck was parked by it, and two men were standing chatting and smoking. As the car drew near they flung their cigarettes to the ground and tried to look busy.

'Damn them,' muttered Charles Weldon. 'They've been loafing around instead of getting on with the check-up.' He glanced briefly back at Helena.

'Keep the doors locked when I get out. I'll hurry them up.' He looked at his watch. The driver halted the car a few yards away from the truck, and her father got out. Shelley watched him approach the men, who were now busily looking over the small plane, tapping here and there, extremely occupied. She saw him speak to them, and looked at her window. If she could wind that down and shout for help—she took a quick glance at Helena, who was watching her like a hawk.

'Tell me,' Shelley said pleasantly, 'was he really with you last night?'

'Wouldn't you like to know?' Helena smiled.

'Not really. I was just making polite conversation before I leave.' Shelley smiled back at her. 'You look like a tart to me.'

'You bitch!' Helena leaned forward, and Shelley punched her with all her strength and opened the window and yelled: 'Help—help—please!'

The driver flung himself back at her and grabbed her, and Shelley brought the comb up and ran it down his face with all the force she could manage. He shouted something and she braced herself against the back of the seat, lifted her feet and kicked him hard on the chin. He went back as if poleaxed, and Helena, still groggy, screamed and dived at Shelley. There was a brief, inglorious struggle in which Shelley grabbed a handful of the other's hair, yanked it back hard, and pushed her other hand under Helena's chin. She was furious now beyond all reason, and the car shook with the force of her assault. She felt Helena go limp, and scrabbled for the door handle out of the open window. The two maintenance men looked alarmed, and she shouted out again: 'Please help——' One began to move towards the car as Shelley managed to open the door and stumbled out on to the ground—then it was as if the world went mad.

She heard the clamour of a siren, cars' engines coming nearer and nearer, and saw one of the maintenance men knock her father to the ground, and she fell, feeling only now, for the first time, the blow on her face that Helena had managed to get in before being knocked out. The world spun round, then she was being lifted, and held, and Vargen's voice was saying: 'Oh, my darling—my darling——' and she knew then that she must have gone completely mad. The world was blotted out in a whirling rush of golds and blues and exploding stars. . . .

When she came round she was sitting on the ground with Eileen and Victor supporting her, and Vargen kneeling in front of her, dabbing her face with a damp handkerchief. She looked round dazedly to see two police cars, and Vargen's car parked nearby, four police-men putting handcuffs on her father, the driver, and a very groggy Helena, and the two maintenance men talking to another policeman.

'It's all over,' said Vargen. 'You're safe now.'

'How——' she began. 'How——?'

'You were never in any danger, my darling,' he said, and she saw a look in his eyes that she had never seen before, but she scarcely heard his words, because she couldn't look away from him. He helped her gently to her feet, and Victor and Eileen stood up as well, while Vargen held her, supporting her, and said:

'Come and sit in my car.' Victor walked over to where Charles Weldon, his brother, was being held, and began speaking to him. Shelley looked at Vargen, then Eileen, as they walked over to Vargen's car, and Eileen said:

'Excuse me,' and turned away as though she had an overwhelming interest in the plane.

Vargen helped Shelley into the car, nodded at Alfredo, who obediently and silently got out and wandered over to talk to Eileen. Shelley turned to Vargen, and he reached out and put his arm tightly round her.

'It's all right now,' he said. 'They would never have taken you. Those two 'maintenance' men were detectives I hired to watch the plane. I knew your father's every move. I knew he had stayed on Avala when we left, and exactly what he was up to, as soon as he enquired about hiring a plane. He has been watched every minute of every day since he arrived. And you also were watched every moment today, from the minute you left Alfredo to the time when that woman stopped to talk to you. As soon as you were taken, I was informed, and I called the airport to arrange the maintenance truck. In any case the plane couldn't have taken off because an essential part of the engine had been removed only three hours ago.'

Shelley lay in his arms, listening, not caring anyway because he was holding her in a way he never had before, speaking in a way he had never spoken before, and nothing else mattered. 'I was so frightened,' she whispered. 'I thought I'd never see you again—and then I knew you wouldn't care anyway——'

He made a small wordless exclamation of pain. 'Oh God!' he said. 'Didn't you know? Last night—when I was ill—can't you guess why?'

'Why? Tell me,' she said.

'Because I had finally found out what your father was up to, what he planned—and in doing so, I had realised I love you. And that hit me harder than anything I've ever had happen to me. I'd been standing in that lounge, just looking out of the window, for three hours when you woke up. I was in a turmoil, knowing you hated me, and knowing you had every reason to hate me——' he groaned. 'How can I ever explain?'

'You're not doing so badly,' she murmured. 'But you're wrong. I thought I hated you—but I loved you at the same time, only I guessed what my father had told you.'

'I knew it wasn't true the first time I made love to you—and then despised myself.' He hugged her. 'I love you, Shelley, I love you very much. I never thought I'd say that to any woman again——' he groaned. 'Oh, my dearest, I would never have put you through this. Don't you see? I didn't want you to go out, but I couldn't tell you why, I didn't want to frighten you.'

'And I thought you were being like my father,' she whispered.

'How stupid I've been! All along. Do you remember that first time I kissed you—in the lounge, after your lunch with Victor and Eileen?'

Shelley looked at him, the memory of pain and rejection coming back so forcibly that she could only nod, not answer.

'You thought—I don't know what you thought, except that I was brutal. But how could you know my feelings then—that I wanted to take you there and then and make love to you?'

'I saw contempt in your eyes,' she whispered.

'Contempt! Oh, God—had you known! I was having to exert every scrap of self-control to hold myself back from you.'

She sighed a little sigh, and Vargen touched her face, his hand trembling, and kissed her. 'Ah, my love,' he whispered, 'soon—soon——' Then he smiled. 'You fought like a tiger. That woman will take a while to recover! And the driver—you knocked him cold.'

'Is it true? Do you know her? She said her name was Helena—I thought the yacht——'

'Helena?' He looked out to see the blonde-haired woman being led away, sullen and struggling, towards one of the police cars. 'Is that her name? I've seen her at some reception, I think, but I've never spoken to her. The boat was named after my mother, Shelley. She was very beautiful, and I painted that picture of her when I was twenty, and she died soon afterwards.' He stroked her hair thoughtfully. 'I'm going to take you away again, for a few days on the yacht. Would you like that? It'll be very different this time, I promise you.' Then he turned to her, and lifted her face gently and looked into her eyes, and his shone with love, were filled with it. Shelley smiled tremulously.

'Yes,' she said very softly, 'I'd like that very much.'

He kissed her very tenderly. 'You have a bruise on your face. We must look after that. I must look after you properly now, for you are very precious to me. Do you know that?'

'I think so,' she murmured.

He hugged her. 'Before we go, I think Victor has something to tell you.' She looked up at him, eyes puzzled.

'What?'

'I think it's better he tells you himself. It may be a shock to you—but, I think, a pleasant one.'

Shelley saw Victor approaching them, hand in hand with Eileen, she saw the concern on his face, and the love, and her heart leapt in her throat. She remembered something he had said about her mother—how he had once clearly loved her, and she knew then, deep down, what she was to be told. She turned and saw the man she had always considered to be her father being led away, a shattered man, and it was like the last pieces of a jigsaw falling into place. She said softly: 'I think I've realised something I should have known long ago.'

Vargen kissed her hair very tenderly. 'I am so happy that you came into my life, my darling,' he said. 'You have changed it in so many ways. You've helped me see so much I did not see before—and now, I have a family. Come, let us go and meet them.' He opened the door, and they went out into the sunlight. Shelley ran to Victor and hugged him, sobbing, and he held her and murmured:

'Oh, my dear child, you know.'

Eyes shining, she looked at him. 'I guessed, but only now.' She turned to Vargen and held out her hand, and he came into the little circle, and the four of them stood there, laughing and crying at the same time, in the blazing heat of the day which had now turned to magic. And that was how it would be, from now on.

Make 1981 your best year yet!

Harlequin
Romance Horoscope 1981

★

How to find your most compatible mate!

★

When to plan that romantic rendezvous!

★

**How to attract the man you want!
And much, much more!**

Choose your own special guide—
the book for your zodiac sign.
Find the way to love and happiness
in the coming year!

PLUS **Romance Calendar 1981**
A special guide for those in love!

Harlequin
Romance Horoscope

Available now at your favorite store!

SPECIAL

Harlequin Romance Treasury Book Offer

This superb Romance Treasury is yours at little or <u>no</u> cost.

3 exciting, full-length Romance novels in one beautiful hard-cover book.

**Introduce yourself to
Harlequin Romance Treasury.
The most beautiful books you've ever seen!**

Cover and spine of each volume features a distinctive gilt design.
An elegant bound-in ribbon bookmark completes the classic design.
No detail has been overlooked to make Romance Treasury
volumes as beautiful and lasting as the stories they contain.
What a delightful way to enjoy the very best and most popular
Harlequin romances again and again!

Here's how to get your volume NOW!

MAIL IN	$	GET
2 SPECIAL PROOF-OF-PURCHASE SEALS*	PLUS $1 U.S.	ONE BOOK
5 SPECIAL PROOF-OF-PURCHASE SEALS*	PLUS 50¢ U.S.	ONE BOOK
8 SPECIAL PROOF-OF-PURCHASE SEALS*	FREE	ONE BOOK

*Special proof-of-purchase seal from inside back cover of all specially marked Harlequin "Let Your Imagination Fly Sweepstakes" volumes.
No other proof-of-purchase accepted.

ORDERING DETAILS:

Print your name, address, city, state or province, zip or postal code on the coupon below or a plain 3" x 5" piece of paper and together with the special proof-of-purchase seals and check or money order (no stamps or cash please) as indicated. Mail to:

**HARLEQUIN
ROMANCE TREASURY
BOOK OFFER
P.O. BOX 1399
MEDFORD, N.Y. 11763, U.S.A.**

Make check or money order payable to: Harlequin Romance Treasury Offer. Allow 3 to 4 weeks for delivery.

Special offer expires: June 30, 1981.

PLEASE PRINT

Name

Address

Apt. No.

City

State/ Prov.

Zip/Postal Code

Let Your Imagination Fly Sweepstakes

Rules and Regulations:

NO PURCHASE NECESSARY

1. Enter the Let Your Imagination Fly Sweepstakes 1, 2 or 3 as often as you wish. Mail each entry form separately bearing sufficient postage. Specify the sweepstake you wish to enter on the outside of the envelope. Mail a completed entry form or, your name, address, and telephone number printed on a plain 3"x 5" piece of paper to:

HARLEQUIN LET YOUR IMAGINATION FLY SWEEPSTAKES,
P.O. BOX 1280, MEDFORD, N.Y. 11763 U.S.A.

2. Each completed entry form must be accompanied by I Let Your Imagination Fly proof-of-purchase seal from the back inside cover of specially marked Let Your Imagination Fly Harlequin books (or the words "Let Your Imagination Fly" printed on a plain 3"x 5" piece of paper. Specify by number the Sweepstakes you are entering on the outside of the envelope.

3. The prize structure for each sweepstake is as follows:

Sweepstake 1 - North America

Grand Prize winner's choice: a one-week trip for two to either Bermuda; Montreal, Canada; or San Francisco. 3 Grand Prizes will be awarded (min. approx. retail value $1,375. U.S., based on Chicago departure) and 4,000 First Prizes: scarves by nik nik, worth $14. U.S. each. All prizes will be awarded.

Sweepstake 2 - Caribbean

Grand Prize winner's choice: a one-week trip for two to either Nassau, Bahamas; San Juan, Puerto Rico; or St. Thomas, Virgin Islands. 3 Grand Prizes will be awarded. (Min. approx. retail value $1,650. U.S., based on Chicago departure) and 4,000 First Prizes: simulated diamond pendants by Kenneth Jay Lane, worth $15. U.S. each. All prizes will be awarded.

Sweepstake 3 - Europe

Grand Prize winner's choice: a one-week trip for two to either London, England; Frankfurt, Germany; Paris, France; or Rome, Italy. 3 Grand Prizes will be awarded. (Min. approx. retail value $2,800. U.S., based on Chicago departure) and 4,000 First Prizes: 1/2 oz. bottles of perfume, BLAZER by Anne Klein (Retail value over $30. U.S.). All prizes will be awarded.

Grand trip prizes will include coach round-trip airfare for two persons from the nearest commercial airport serviced by Delta Air Lines to the city as designated in the prize, double occupancy accommodation at a first- class or medium hotel, depending on vacation, and $500. U.S. spending money. Departure taxes, visas, passports, ground transportation to and from airports will be the responsibility of the winners.

4. To be eligible, Sweepstakes entries must be received as follows:
Sweepstake 1 Entries received by February 28, 1981
Sweepstake 2 Entries received by April 30, 1981
Sweepstake 3 Entries received by June 30, 1981
Make sure you enter each Sweepstake separately since entries will not be carried forward from one Sweepstake to the next.

The odds of winning will be determined by the number of entries received in each of the three sweepstakes. Canadian residents, in order to win any prize, will be required to first correctly answer a time-limited skill-testing question, to be posed by telephone, at a mutually convenient time.

5. Random selections to determine Sweepstake 1, 2 or 3 winners will be conducted by Lee Krost Associates, an independent judging organization whose decisions are final. Only one prize per family, per sweepstake. Prizes are non-transferable and non-refundable and no substitutions will be allowed. Winners will be responsible for any applicable federal, state and local taxes. Trips must be taken during normal tour periods before June 30, 1982. Reservations will be on a space-available basis. Airline tickets are non-transferable, non-refundable and non-redeemable for cash.

6. The Let Your Imagination Fly Sweepstakes is open to all residents of the United States of America and Canada, (excluding the Province of Quebec) except employees and their immediate families of Harlequin Enterprises Ltd., its advertising agencies, Marketing & Promotion Group Canada Ltd. and Lee Krost Associates, Inc., the independent judging company. Winners may be required to furnish proof of eligibility. Void wherever prohibited or restricted by law. All federal, state, provincial and local laws apply.

7. For a list of trip winners, send a stamped, self-addressed envelope to:
Harlequin Trip Winners List, P.O. Box 1401, MEDFORD, N.Y. 11763 U.S.A.
Winners lists will be available after the last sweepstake has been conducted and winners determined.
NO PURCHASE NECESSARY.

Let Your Imagination Fly Sweepstakes

OFFICIAL ENTRY FORM

Please enter me in Sweepstake No. _____

Please print:

Name _____

Address _____

Apt. No.	City

State/ Prov.	Zip/Postal Code

Telephone No.   area code
( )

MAIL TO:
HARLEQUIN LET YOUR
IMAGINATION FLY SWEEPSTAKE No. _____
P.O. BOX 1280,
MEDFORD, N.Y. 11763 U.S.A.

(Please specify by number, the Sweepstake you are entering.)